BRENNUS

Immortal Highlander, Clan Skaraven Book 1

HAZEL HUNTER

HH ONLINE

✦✦✦

Hazel loves hearing from readers!
You can contact her at the links below.

Website: hazelhunter.com

Facebook:
business.facebook.com/HazelHunterAuthor

Newsletter: HazelHunter.com/news

I send newsletters with details on new releases,
special offers, and other bits of news related to
my writing. You can sign up here!

Chapter One

BEING A REDHEAD in Scotland helped Althea Jarden blend in with the locals, at least until she spoke. Although she'd lost most of her southern accent while working on her Ph.D. at Cornell, whatever she said broadcast her as an American. Fortunately, no one held that against her. The Scots she met were more curious as to why she wasn't out shopping, taking a tour of Fort George, or snapping photos of Loch Ness in hopes of spotting its infamous monster.

"I'm just here for the ferns," she told the innkeeper and his wife as she checked out at their front desk. "I'm a field botanist working for the University of Glasgow. We're researching hart's-tongue fern's chemical components and mechanisms of action." When the couple's jaws sagged she quickly added, "I collect and test plants to make new medicines."

"Och, like my Gran does," the wife said, looking relieved. She nudged her husband. "Jamie here got a huge keeker when the Frazier lad come at him bleezin' in the pub." She drew a large circle in front of her own eye. "What you'd call a black eye, I reckon. My Gran's parsley and tea poultice took down the swelling in a snap."

The man scowled. "Aye, and it reeked like an alky's carpet, Deb." He handed Althea the receipt for her room charges, and asked, "Where are you off to now, Miss?"

She shouldered her carryall. "My next stop is the Isle of Skye, and then back to Glasgow."

"On Skye you'll no' be let near the Trotternish ridge," he said and nodded past her at the old television in the lobby, which was showing a newscast. "They barricaded all the trails last night after the Old Man of Storr crumbled. Naught but a pile of rubble left, they say."

"How terrible," Althea said. The rock formation was a popular tourist spot, and one of the most-photographed places in Scotland. "What caused it to collapse? An earthquake?"

"They dinnae ken yet," Deb told her. "But this rock expert they had 'round blamed a big sun surge that hit us before dawn. Something about the magnetics, wasn't it, Jamie?"

"Geomagnetics, and he called it a solar flare," her husband corrected. "It's meddled with the satellites, and disrupted electronics and signals all over the highlands. He said it's likely to last for hours, Miss, so your mobile may no' work until afternoon."

"Thanks for the warning," Althea said and smiled her good-bye to the couple.

She hadn't planned to visit the Storr while she was on the island. The ferns she wanted grew in a glen near the Black Cuillin. But the collapse would attract plenty of press. Cameras and reporters ranked at the top of her "Avoid" list.

Being the only child of dead rock stars had turned her into a media magnet for life.

Outside the inn Althea stowed the carryall in her rental car, and then walked down to have one last look at the loch. Behind the vivid ambers, oranges and scarlets of the autumn-painted trees the sky streamed with puffy ribbons of cloud. The dappled surface of the waters reflected the surrounding beauty like a master impressionist intent on capturing every hue. Since no one else was braving the early morning chill, Althea felt as if she had Scotland all to herself.

Wouldn't that be something? she thought, smiling a little. No towns or tourists, cars or roads—just her and nature, the way it used to be growing up on her uncle's farm. She'd been so happy there, away from her famous parents and the endless drama of their love-hate relationship.

As the founding members of the Nighthood, Will and Sharan Scarlet had headlined the world's most famous Gothic rock band. With their blazing red hair and tattered bohemian style, they had set trends all over the globe. But it had been Will's haunting lyrics and Sharan's operatic soprano that had catapulted them to the top. By the time their third album went triple-platinum, Will took his place among the top-selling songwriters of the century, while Sharan became a global idol and fashion icon as well as the most influential voice of her generation. Considered the most romantic couple in rock, the Scarlets had been utterly obsessed with each other.

The only hiccup in their epic love story performance had been Althea.

What the hell is this? Althea's mother had shrieked when she found the plane tickets to Georgia. *You're dumping the kid at your brother's place? Why?*

Will had bellowed right back at her. *Her name is Ally, and you can't take care of her, Shar. Christ, do you even look at her anymore? She's so thin I can count her ribs.*

She never wants to eat anything. Sharan had lit a cigarette and waved her beringed hand in the air. *Don't you blame me. The idiot roadies are supposed to feed her.*

So, we let the crew raise our daughter? What kind of mother are you?

Her mother's famous emerald-green eyes narrowed. *Like you're father of the year, you shit.*

As usual, the argument had escalated into a raucous, vicious fight, and ended with the Scarlets in the bedroom at the back of the tour bus. Althea remembered the details only because it was the last time she had seen her parents. Their studio manager took her from the bus and flew with her from Houston to Atlanta. From there he'd driven her to her uncle's farm in the heart of Georgia's dairy and logging country.

Gene Jarden turned out to be an older, leaner version of his brother, a lifelong bachelor, and a complete stranger to five-year-old Althea. After the Jarden's studio manager hurried off to catch his plane, the farmer had just stood there looking her over for a long time.

"You got a little of me, didn't you?" He crouched down so she could see the same, crystal-blue eyes she saw in the mirror every morning. "It'll be fine now, Althea. You just need a bit of fresh air and sunshine. You like peaches?"

Too terrified to say anything, she nodded.

Her uncle straightened and held out his hand. "Then you'd best come and help me pick some."

Gene's peach orchard covered three acres, and as they walked through the rows of the wide-topped trees with their blushing golden fruit he talked about the farm. He let her choose her peach, and lifted her up in his arms so she could pluck it off the branch. Althea couldn't remember ever doing anything like that. All she knew was that nothing before or since that day had tasted better than her first bite of that juicy, sun-warmed fruit. She wouldn't have become a botanist without her uncle and his orchard. Both of them had changed her life forever.

The sound of her smart phone ringing brought Althea back to the present, although when she saw who was calling on the display she frowned. She hadn't spoken to Gregory Davis since a year ago, when they'd gone their separate ways.

"Hello?"

"It's Greg. How's Inverness?" Without waiting for an answer, he said, "I'm flying to London today for a lecture series, and I heard you were over there. Any chance we could get together? I'm staying at Claridge's."

Throwing her phone in Loch Ness would be the most appropriate response, she thought.

"London is a bit of a haul for a one-night stand."

"Same old Ally," her ex said, and chuckled. "Still as cold as ice. I swear, you've got liquid nitrogen for blood."

She hated being called Ally—another reason she'd broken it off with him. "Anything else before I hang up?"

"Yes. I want you back," Greg said. "I know you said no strings, but I thought we really had something, Ally. I miss you."

Althea imagined him reclined in the executive chair in his office, his tie loose and his dark blond hair falling over his smooth brow and dark brown eyes. He'd smell clean and warm, with a hint of the pricey cologne he liked to wear. By tonight she could be in that hotel bed with him, naked and enjoying his gym-toned body.

The problem was that she knew what the man actually wanted. For now, more sex, but also another chance to lure her into a relationship.

A traditionalist at heart, Greg would eventually talk her into marriage. After the honeymoon, he'd also persuade her to give up her work, so he could focus on his agritech career, where the real money was. In twenty years she imagined she'd have a lovely house, charity work, two kids in prep school, and a husband with the traditional mid-life crisis. He'd divorce her, buy a convertible, and move in with a lover young enough to be his daughter. Meanwhile, their kids would grow up and go. Althea suspected she'd end up middle-aged and alone, with nothing to show but an empty nest and ruined dreams.

Althea would have told him that, too, but her uncle had taught her to be polite, particularly when she was this pissed off. "No, thank you. Enjoy your time in London." Her hand shook as she shut off the phone.

The anger slowly subsided as she walked back to the car. She hated when her emotions boiled over, but she couldn't blame Greg for this. Loneliness had driven her into his arms, but she'd lingered too long. Obviously he'd developed feelings and expectations she couldn't reciprocate.

Or maybe she was just over-reacting to what had been a transatlantic booty call, dressed up like a romantic appeal.

Althea didn't know. She never got emotionally involved with men. Oh, she'd always been passionate—sometimes to the point where she was overwhelmed by her own desires. Her self-imposed isolation brought on terrible bouts of loneliness, and she tried to channel her needs and frustrations into her work. Sometimes it wasn't enough, and she was tempted to do stupid things like her fling with Greg.

No doubt her lack of romantic interest did make her seem cold, but she needed that facade. It assured she wouldn't end up in some obsessive-abusive relationship like her parents. She had no intention of ever falling in love. Given her family history, she simply couldn't take the risk.

At least Althea had the work to keep her occupied. She touched the crystal heart pendant hidden under her shirt. A gift from her uncle for her sixteenth birthday, she'd worn it every day since his death. It reminded her of his love, and her calling.

With its endless woodlands, and the rare ferns they protected, Scotland had enormous potential for new finds. Today, she thought as she climbed into her rental, she'd discover something. Something that would make her forget that, without her uncle, she was alone in the world. She would focus on the work and, as usual, rely on herself.

Chapter Two

A S THE HIGHLANDS flew by in a blur, Murdina Stroud relished the sunlight that flashed on her face. Nature had not changed in this new age, but the rest of the world seemed altered almost beyond recognition. From the odd garments she wore to the contraption called a car, everything seemed so complicated and contrived. This was not her world. Why had she been awakened here?

The trews and tunic she'd taken from the female villager on Skye perplexed her. Why did women dress like men? She would have worn her own robes, but being trapped in the Storr for two thousand years had reduced them to dust. She had emerged from the rubble as naked as a newborn. Apt, for this was a day of rebirth as well as release from imprisonment. She and Hendry had returned to the world.

Today would be the beginning of everything. She had to remember that.

Looking at the man driving in the front of the car made Murdina want to scream. They'd left his woman naked and unconscious back on Skye while compelling him to bring them to the mainland. He had offered no resistance to the simple spell Hendry had cast to control him, but his strangeness gnawed at her. If she had a dagger to open his veins, she could watch him die. Spilled blood made such pretty patterns on flesh.

"You set fire to my heart, beauty mine," Hendry Greum said, wrapping his slim hand around hers. His white-streaked silver hair brushed her cheek as he leaned closer. "I thought never again to see you."

Gazing into her lover's eyes brought Murdina out of her ruinous haze. Every color of the forest's shadows lay in Hendry's deep-set hazel irises, framed by frosted gray lashes. Like her, he hadn't aged a day since they had been imprisoned. Now that they had awakened as immortals, neither of them would ever again change. Hendry's angular jaw and slightly crooked nose would remain just as they were forever.

Her brief joy charred to bleak wrath as she recalled why eternal life had been bestowed on them: to keep their souls from escaping their bodies and the Storr.

"They took everything." The words came out of her with a ragged rasp. "If you hadnae been beside me—"

"Naught could keep me from you," he murmured, kissing the space between her brows. "'Tis behind us, Murdina mine. Now we must free our *caraidean*, our friends as they'd say in this age. Then we must go back." The shadows in his eyes deepened. "Bhaltair Flen and his tribe will answer for what they have done."

"Aye." She embraced him, grateful for his unshakeable resolve. The way he stroked her back made her wish to be naked again, to feel his touch on her skin. It kept her from remembering the endless, yawning dark from which she could not escape.

"Master, this is Corrimony," the damp-faced driver said, and looked at them in the sliver of mirror by his head as the conveyance slowed to a stop. "You'll no' be able to visit the cairn. They've closed the site."

Hendry peered at the yellow-and-black striped barricade and large, lettered sign blocking the footbridge over the stream. "Tell me the meaning of those words."

"NOSAS stands for the North of Scotland Archaeological Society. They're having a dig here to uncover something buried near the old cairn. Been on the telly box for weeks." His hand shook as he pointed at other mortals working inside a flimsy wire fence. "See the men 'round that pit? They'll no' let you near it."

Murdina spotted shattered casing stones piled around the pit, and a wide curve of blackened wood supported by thick stumps. "They've uncovered it. How thoughtful." Perhaps she'd allow some of them to die quickly.

Hendry gripped the mortal's shoulder. Power flared bright green beneath his palm before it funneled into the man's mouth.

When he released him, the mortal climbed out of the conveyance and went to the back to open a hatch there.

As Hendry helped her out of the car, Murdina eyed the gathered mortals. None of them was druid kind. "Naught to concern us here. Shall I kill them all?"

"If they meddle, that one will attend to them." Her lover nodded at their driver, who now held a metal rod with a curled end. "Now come, miracle mine. Our *caraidean* sense our presence and grow impatient."

She walked arm-in-arm with Hendry around the barricade and across the footbridge, glancing back to assure the driver followed. Two scowling workers came to meet them halfway between the road and the pit. The older of the two held up a callused hand in a stopping gesture.

"Did you no' read the sign?" the younger man demanded. "Site's closed. Leave."

"No' yet," Hendry murmured to the driver before he regarded the unruly mortal. "We wished to ask how you located the wood henge."

"We were using ground-penetrating radar

equipment to survey the site when we found it," the older mortal said, and frowned. "Who told you it was a henge? We've no' released that information to the public."

"And the casing stones?" Hendry gestured at the rubble being piled around the pit. He sidestepped the men, making them turn toward him. "How did you break through them?"

"We found them goosed this morning," the younger man snapped. "Now quit your blethering or we'll have the police come and—"

His words dissolved into a sharp cry as he dropped to his knees and toppled into the grass, the back of his neck streaking with blood.

The older worker stumbled back, but not far enough to avoid the driver's second blow, which felled him next to his moaning companion.

Seeing the gleam of the wet red excited Murdina. "Let me have them."

"'Twill take too long to kill them all." Hendry lifted his hands, his power growing bright as it gathered and seethed over his palms. "In terror and silence be, away from mine and me."

Murdina watched his power divide into dozens of glowing green orbs. They flew forward to burst over the mortals around the pit. As soon as the magic touched them, the mortals dropped their tools without a word and fled.

"Stand guard," Hendry told the driver. To Murdina he said, "I sense the traces of Flen's broken enchantment. The conclave had him use sunlight to power the imprisonment spells here and on Skye." His upper lip curled. "How predictable."

"Yet the sun still shines," Murdina said, gazing at the sky. A strange resonance still lingered around them. "And the light trembles."

"'Twas a sun storm," her lover said. He grimaced as he shielded his eyes and followed her gaze. "In our time such couldnae affect such enchantments. The sky now is thinner, and the air tainted by smoke and more I dinnae ken."

He led her to the edge of the pit, where the mortals had removed most of the shattered stone casings and burial soil. The wide oval of tall oak tree posts appeared intact, still joined together by an enormous ring of ash wood inlaid with polished cabochons of dark topaz. Fragments of long-dead mistletoe vines still wrapped around each of the fifty-six posts. Nothing grew in the earth around the henge. Bhaltair Flen had salted the burial soil so much it resembled blood-stained snow.

Murdina had expected the worst, but to see their *caraidean's* prison brought back all the old pain. "Can you free them?"

"With your power joined to mine, aye." He clasped her hands between his. "Open for me, best beloved mine, and give me all."

An unexpected shame filled her. "I'm no' as once I was for you."

"Nor I." He brought her hands to his mouth, kissing the center of each palm before pressing them against his chest. "I dinnae care. With you I am everything, my lady."

The love in his eyes soothed Murdina as she lowered the wards that contained her own power. As Hendry's magic drew on hers, she felt the changes their long exile had wrought in him. His anger had grown like hers: a constant, boiling fury, fed by his desires to see those responsible suffer. The clarity that had once guided his clever mind now lay behind a fortress of icy, ruthless ambition. Just when she thought they had both gone mad, his feelings for her engulfed her.

All fell away as she wrapped herself in those deep, eventide shadows. "My poor love," she whispered.

He caressed her cheek. "'Twill be as I promised. Once the reckoning is finished, the world belongs to us and the *caraidean.*"

Hendry reached out over the pit, her hands still entwined with his, and closed his eyes. Murdina felt his lean body shake as he gathered and combined their powers to fuel the spell he murmured. Popping and splintering sounds rose from the pit. In the next instant the dark brown gems hurled upward from the warping ring of ash wood. As the last words of the incantation left her lover's lips, the circle cracked and fell away from the oak posts. The massive wood columns groaned, the pitch spiraling upward, until loud cracks split the air. As the oak posts ruptured into halves, the immortal spirits within escaped.

A soft rumble spread out over the land, like the distant roar of an immense beast uncaged.

Murdina watched the *caraidean* emerge from the henge, her fear fading as awe swelled in her breast. Each of the fifty-six spirits rose from the pit as a phantom of what they had once been: massive totems carved of sacred oak. Now they hovered in the air, shimmering and bodiless. They stretched up as they had in life, more than seven ells tall, four times the size of a human. Their broadness invoked the mightiness of the massive trunks from which they had been hewn, and their limbs bulged just as thick and unyielding.

Nothing that had ever walked the earth could match their magnificence.

"We didnae forget," Hendry called out to them.

Closing his eyes and murmuring under his breath, he cast a little known spell. From each post, a splinter rose up from the pit to hover above it. With a flick of his hand, he scattered the fragments over the grass beneath the phantom oaks, which slowly descended and enveloped them. The slivers of wood swelled and elongated, taking on the shape of the totems they had once been. Now Murdina added her own magic to their efforts, casting a wide swath of transmuting power over the giants, which shrank them down as they took on human form. When the intense light dwindled and vanished, fifty-six enormous warriors stood on the other side of the pit, each watching them.

"Welcome back, my friends." Hendry bowed so low his brow nearly touched his knees.

Murdina had no skirts to sweep back into a proper curtsey, but she did her best in the strange garments. "We came as soon as the sun storm freed us."

One of the largest of the transformed hobbled to the front, rocking unsteadily on his new legs as he came around the pit. The ground beneath their feet trembled with each step he took.

"Gratitude," he said in a creaky voice. As he came to a stop in front of them, he touched his own jaw and ran his hand over his neck, producing an eerie grating sound. "You remade us. Why, Hendry Greum of the Wood Dream?"

Hearing the name of their slaughtered people spoken after two thousand years, even in the giant's grating, unnatural voice, made Murdina clutch her lover's arm. If the immortal *caraidean* remembered them, then they had not changed.

"Aon," Hendry said, "we must go back and punish the Dawn Fire tribe for what they did. Then we would begin the reckoning." He knelt before the giant. "For this, we ask your help. If 'tis no' your wish, I shall restore you to your true forms, and bid you farewell."

The giant lifted and turned his hand to inspect it before he offered it to Hendry, tugging him to his feet. "We shall return with you for the punishing and the reckoning."

Murdina glanced at the other giants, who were testing their new limbs by milling about in an uneven circle. They would be clumsy until they became accustomed to their new forms, and then they would be unstoppable. She would have to ask Hendry to save Bhaltair Flen for her, however. She had spent several centuries in the darkness planning what she would do once the old meddler's soul was in her hands, and an easy death would not be his. Indeed, what she would see him suffer would make being trapped in the Storr seem like a benevolence.

"The druids used a portal to put us in the henge," Aon said and stretched out a long, bulky arm toward the stream. "There."

"The ancient cairns here remain intact," Hendry said, "so too may the portal." He slipped his arm around Murdina's waist. "Shall we begin our new journey, druidess mine?"

As they made their way to the secluded oak grove, she wanted to skip beside the sparkling stream. But they slowed when they neared the sacred grove. Waist-high weeds choked the clearing in the center, and the trees surrounding it had grown into each other. Most of their twisted, interlaced branches had died, reminding Murdina of funeral pyre wood. She tugged on her lover's arm until he halted just outside the grove.

"Bhaltair may have left a trap for the *caraidean*, should they escape the henge."

"No snare magic here, druidess," Aon said

and gestured toward one of the other giants, who had a deep scar running down the center of his face. "Tri, open the portal."

The big warrior trudged through the oaks and stopped on the edge of the clearing. He reached down to touch the ground—but nothing. Then he slammed his fist into it but still there was naught. After several other attempts that included his feet and head, he came out and stopped before Aon.

"They willnae permit," Tri creaked in his surreal voice. He glared back at the overgrown oaks. "Silent to me."

Aon sent more of the giants to test the portal, yet none could open it. At last the leader of the *caraidean* tried himself to gain entry, but the clearing remained closed.

"This grove cannae remember us," the giant finally said and surveyed the trees. "They came up after the old trees burned."

"Mayhap they dinnae recognize you in your altered form," Hendry said, and drew Murdina with him to enter the clearing. "Follow us once we open the portal," he called back to Aon, but when they stepped into the center, the ground did not open.

More disturbing to Murdina was how the oaks remained still and quiet with two druid kind in their midst. "Surely they cannae refuse us."

Hendry dropped down and pressed his hands to the soil for a long moment before he rose. "More of Flen's scheme. None of us can use the portal."

She realized what he meant. "The oaks cannae sense us as druid kind." Panic shot through her as she stared at the ground. "We'll be trapped here."

"No," Aon declared. His cold shadow stretched over them. "We begin the reckoning here. Now." He lifted his huge arm and splayed his hand against the wind. A thick mist released into the air that then silvered. It showed an opaque image of a young woman among trees. "There, walking in the forest. A female of the Dawn Fire. She shall open the portal for us."

"So, druid kind persist," Hendry said and spat on the ground. "But this era is full of flimsy creatures, so we shall need more than one. How many other druid kind females do you sense near us?"

Aon raised both hands and turned in a slow circle. The air around grew dense with a haze of particles emanating from his form, and took on a woody, sharp scent. At last he regarded Hendry. "Four others may be taken."

The particles Aon had released turned silvery as the first one had, and showed images of the females he had located.

Hendry studied all of them and smiled at one in particular. "Lady mine, do you see what I do?"

"By the gods," Murdina whispered as she gripped his hand tightly. "How can it be?"

"By the gods," her lover echoed, and kissed her brow. To Aon he said, "They'll serve our purpose. Only remember, we need them alive."

"As you will, so we do."

Aon rejoined the other giants, choosing four among them to walk out of the grove.

Murdina and Hendry followed, and she leaned against her lover as the five *caraidean* sank into the ground. Once they had submerged completely, raised ridges of earth began to streak out in different directions, toppling trees and smashing through fences.

"So, it begins," Hendry said, sounding very satisfied as he glanced around them. "'Twill be a very different world when we're finished."

She nodded. "Once we kill all the humans, 'twill be ours to remake."

Chapter Three

⁂

SHATTERING LIGHT POURED over Chieftain Brennus Skaraven, scrolling over his skin and dragging him from the darkness. He opened his eyes to find himself standing knee-deep in snow atop the high, flat plateau of the *Am Monadh Ruadh*. Winter had come to the red hills to freeze the wellsprings into mirrored coins. Ice veiled the granite tors, making the ancient rock pillars glitter with the false promise of silver ore.

He could not remember coming here.

Yesterday he had led his men against the *famhairean*, the giants even more terrifying than the Skaraven Clan. The battle had been brutal, savage, and had ended in darkness, but not in this place. They'd fought in summer, not winter. And while the bitter climes of the highlands had rarely troubled Brennus, thanks to his towering, muscled-padded form, here he felt no chill at all. The snow clinging to his powerful legs might have just as well been sand.

The dead dinnae grow cold.

As Brennus looked up he saw five ravens circling through the sun's tremulous beams. The ink on his chest should have responded to the birds with surging power. But there was only the faintest crackle of his raven battle spirit, as if it were far away. When he knelt to offer proper reverence, the black birds hurtled down, only to dissolve like so many phantoms. His lips drew into a hard line.

Tree-knower tricks.

He rose from the drift and drew his sword, his bicep bunching under his dark cloak as he held the heavy, razor-sharp blade ready.

"Show yourselves."

His deep voice rumbled around him in muffled echoes, but no one appeared.

Brennus's big hand knotted around his blade hilt until his knuckles whitened. He recalled everything that had befallen him: the hard life, endless battle, the brief taste of freedom, and then the final sacrifice. He could not be in the highlands. He'd died yesterday, as had his entire clan. The man who had been Brennus Skaraven lay rotting somewhere with them. The unanswered wrongs that seethed in his heart boiled out of him in a furious bellow to the gods.

"*What do you facking want of me?*"

Without warning the snow beneath his boots dropped away, and Brennus fell again. He smashed his fists against the sides of the dark, whirling tunnel, but he could find no handhold or even slow his plunge. Beneath him he saw an ocean of white stars laced with golden magic, but when he landed he found himself crouching in a bed of thick ferns.

"Oh, wonderful," a young, elated female voice said. "You're going to do great things for us."

Across from him not a hand reach away knelt a slender, flame-haired lass. As Brennus stared at her, the oddness of her faded trews and heavy plaid coat perplexed him. She wore some kind of satchel against her back. But it was being so close to her and not hampered by

chains, that made him hardly dare to breathe.
She paid no heed to him as she plucked the
feathery greens and stowed them in odd sacks
made of thin glass that moved as fabric would.

What new trick was this?

Brennus could not utter a word. All Skaraven had been forbidden to speak to females.
But to look at her filled him with wonder.
Surely, she belonged to a king, for she had the
delicate, unmarked skin of high nobility. Her
uncovered hair had been tied back from the
lovely oval of her face, and flashed with all the
colors of candlelit copper. As she worked, she
pursed her lips, as soft and curvy as flame
flower petals, to kiss the air. Her downcast eyes
remained hidden, but the sweep of her sable
brows and gold-tipped eyelashes promised
something rare and treasured. She wore a
heart-shaped crystal on a fine silver necklace,
both of a like he had never before seen.

The beauty that filled his eyes also made
his gut knot. Gods, who had been mad enough
to let such a splendid creature roam the highlands alone?

She frowned as she pressed aside some
fronds to examine the ground beneath them,

and pressed her palm atop the soil. "Can't be. Jamie said it wasn't an earthquake."

Her strange accent and manner of speaking finally registered. She sounded neither Caledonian nor Pritani to Brennus. He knew nothing of the peoples across the sea, so she might be Francian or a Gaul. The soft timber of her voice made heat bloom in his chest, just beneath his skinwork, which startled him anew. His battle spirit had never once responded to the presence of a female.

All of his confusion scattered as the ground shook beneath him. A mound of earth rapidly piled up at her back. Without thinking he abandoned the old forbiddance and shouted, "Behind you, the *famhair*."

The lass didn't react to his warning. Two huge wooden hands shot out of the soil and seized her by the arms. Her head snapped up and her eyes, the clear blue of sky topaz, went wide as she screamed.

"*No,*" Brennus shouted.

But when he lunged for the female his hands passed through her flesh. He roared his fury as the giant dragged her into the earth. He hurled himself after her into the mound, and became engulfed. The soil piled higher and higher, collapsing on top of him and burying him deep. Brennus fought to free himself, dragging his arms through the shifting earth and ramming his fists above him. Dirt exploded over and around him as he punched his way out of the loose, cold soil, and hoisted himself to his feet.

His raven buckler, now as badly cracked and silvered as bog-wood, tore from its rotted leather straps and fell away from his wide chest. A damp, icy breeze rushed over his bare body and shed the sharp-sweet scent of mistletoe flowers, prodding his temper. He saw nearly a hundred druids standing in a wide oval and watching as the ground shook and heaved. Earth fountained up in violent sprays as dozens of other tall, powerful men clawed their way out of the ground, each warrior as naked as their chieftain. The only thing each wore was a wooden ring carved from sacred oaks. Though blackened by time, each still held the likeness of a raven.

Brennus didn't have to look at their faces to know who they were. Since boyhood he could feel the other men of the Skaraven

Clan. He held up his right fist, brandishing his clan ring.

"Bràithrean an fhithich," he shouted in the old tongue. *Brethren of the raven.*

As his brothers echoed their chieftain's call to arms, they quickly fell into their ranks on either side of him.

This was not where they had died, either, Brennus thought. Nor were the tree-knowers that now encircled it the same who had sent them into battle. Their unfamiliar, dark blue robes concealed their faces with hoods.

Aye, but he'd been right in guessing this their work.

"War Master," Brennus said, keeping his gaze locked on their watchers. "Counsel."

The command brought Cadeyrn, Brennus's second, to his left side. Soil still pelted the Skaraven War Master's broad shoulders and powerful chest, and his sun-streaked umber mane hung down to his waist. He looked, as ever, ready to kill something.

"One hundred strong," Cadeyrn murmured for his ears alone as he kept his fierce bronze eyes fixed on the *dru-wids.* "No wounds or garb. Seventy-seven tree-knowers enclose the field. The *famhairean* have vanished."

Brennus knew the giants would not have willing left the battle, and as he scanned the land for their tracks he saw more disturbing signs. He recognized the river bordering the land to the west was the Enrick, but its course had subtly altered. The oaks at the forest's edge he recalled as saplings had somehow grown into colossal trees. Beyond the river the rocky slopes of the mountains had rounded and spread, as if melting back into the earth. Knots of heather patches and thick grasses now entirely covered the floodplain's bare black soil. As he turned his head, Brennus felt his own night-dark hair brush the small of his back, and recalled how he and the clan had shaved their heads bare before engaging the giants.

All of it told him that more than a day had passed since their deaths.

He glanced down at the sword he still gripped, but it, too, had changed greatly. Rust and soil encased the crumbling iron blade, so thickly that he could no longer make out the lines of the fuller. His Weapons Master,

Kanyth, had forged the sword for him only last winter, and yet it looked as if it had been buried for centuries. But why did he hold the blade when the clan stood unarmed?

Chieftains are always put in the ground with their swords.

One of the tree-knowers used a cane as he left the circle to hobble toward Brennus. Several others carrying piles of folded trews and tunics followed. Behind them, four hauled a low, long cart filled with boots, belts, and thick checkered cloths in every color.

Beside him Cadeyrn's stance shifted from observer to defender. "They carry no weapons."

"They dinnae need them," Brennus reminded him.

The lame *dru-wid* halted a short distance away, and held up a gnarled hand to stop the others trailing him. "Chieftain Brennus, I am Bhaltair Flen, headman of the Dawn Fire tribe." He pulled back his hood to reveal a gaunt, wrinkled face. His piercing dark eyes remained averted from the clan's nudity, as did all the other druids' gazes. "We welcome your return to the mortal realm."

Bhaltair Flen had been a young man with a different face when last they'd met, which meant at least a lifetime had passed. That they now slurred their race's name together hinted at more than one. Temper burned in Brennus, as hot as a whiskey-soaked torch, but he kept it off his face.

"What have you done now?" Brennus demanded.

The old man gestured toward the garb his people held. "Might we first clothe you and your men?"

Like the property they'd once been, Brennus thought. "You'll do naught for us."

After Brennus raised his hand to signal his first-ranked, the nine clansmen strode forward to retrieve the garb and cart. They efficiently distributed the clothing and boots among the other men before dressing. Cadeyrn left and returned with two sets, placing one on the ground beside the chieftain before donning the other.

Brennus made no move to dress himself. "Explain, Tree-Knower."

Temper flared red across Bhaltair's hollowed cheeks, but he kept his tone civil. "As

you ken, we've long owed a debt to the Skaraven Clan."

That explained why none of his people
would look straight at them: what they
cunningly called their *debt*. "How long since
we fell?"

"Some time." The druid cleared his
throat. "The spell we used to awaken you and
your clan bestows immortality. You'll be
stronger and heal faster. You'll no' age, and be
near impossible to kill. You can bond with
water and travel through it to another place
just by thinking of it—"

"How facking long?" Brennus demanded.

The old man recoiled a step before he
regained his composure. "'Tis been twelve
centuries since the day."

None of the clan reacted with sound or
movement, but Brennus could feel their silent
shock like a hail of blunt arrows bouncing off
his back. His own roiled inside him, and if he
set it free now druid blood would spill.

Clenching his jaw, Brennus breathed deep
until he could speak without shouting. "You
didnae do this to repay a debt."

"We did." Bhaltair's stern expression softened. "We've always meant to return you to life, Chieftain. When we did the same with another murdered clan, we created a terrible enemy only recently vanquished. Before we awakened you, we had to be sure 'twould no' happen again."

That much Brennus believed, but then tree-knowers made a practice to add a pinch of truth to every kettle of their lies. "What more?"

Before the old man could reply some of the druids gasped and pointed. Brennus turned his head to see a stag the color of snow standing on the other side of the river. It stood watching them in turn, and then swiveled its head to stare at the chieftain and Bhaltair. A moment later it bounded off and disappeared into the forest.

Brennus felt unmoved. Even if great change was coming, as foretold by the sight of a white stag, the Gods would have to wait their turn.

"Sevenday past, the quislings, Hendry and Murdina, and their giants escaped their imprisonment and returned from the future," Bhaltair said, his face almost as white as the

prophetic deer. "They've encamped somewhere near Beinn Nibheis to take up their evil
work again. Yesterday they slaughtered an
entire village of mortals outside of Lochabar."

A curious ache swelled in Brennus's chest
as he thought of the flame-haired beauty in
the forest. If she had been real, the giants had
already killed her. "Use your tricks on
them again."

"Even if we dared approach them, 'twill
no' work anymore. To prevent the quislings
from reincarnating we– Chieftain, please," he
begged as Brennus turned away. "The details
matter no'. You ken what the giants shall do,
and naught can stop them but the Skaraven.
'Tis why we bred your clan."

The tree-knower spoke of them as if they
yet served as the property of the two Pritani
tribes that had created them. By pairing their
cleverest males and females with their strongest, the *dru-wids* of that time had helped the
tribes deliberately breed one hundred boys to
serve as protectors. As the eldest, Brennus had
been the first to be trained for their cold, grim
lives as indentured warriors. Years of battle
and hardship followed, until a plague had

killed both tribes. That had dissolved the indenture, and the Skaraven had lived for the first time as free men. Too soon that had ended. The druids had come pleading for their help, and sent them to their deaths. Now they had brought them back to use them again.

If nothing else, the old bastart had baws the size of Orkney.

Brennus suddenly knew why the white stag had appeared. A time for change was upon the Skaraven, and as chieftain to see it done fell to him. He handed his rusted blade to Cadeyrn before he tugged on the garb and boots his second had brought for him. His long black hair settled over his shoulders and back like a heavy cloak as he retrieved his sword and faced the dru-wid.

With a single thrust he drove the blade it into the ground between Bhaltair's sandals, where it shattered into a dozen pieces.

"We're no' your slaves anymore," he told the old man. "Clean up your own *cac*."

Chapter Four

ALTHEA SAT IN a corner of the primitive barn and plaited a few pieces of straw onto the braided cord she was making. She hadn't worn a belt, and if her jeans got any looser they'd fall around her ankles. She'd finally figured out how to brush her teeth with a frayed twig sprinkled with salt from a packet in her bag, but her hair hung lank and grimy down her back. Being dirty didn't bother her as much as the horrifying moments that still flashed through her head—moments she still couldn't quite comprehend.

It had happened. She'd been taken. But why? And how had they pulled off the unbelievable way they'd taken her?

Her stomach still clenched whenever she remembered those first, horrifying moments. Like an oversize mole, some creature in the shape of a man had come out of the ground to grab her from behind and pull her into the earth. Then he'd dragged her with him as he'd somehow tunneled beneath the surface. Cuts and bruises still covered her from being hauled through a mass of exploding soil, rocks, and roots. He'd shoved her up into more brutal hands, which had jerked her back into the air. Choking and struggling, Althea had fought for her life, only to be hurled into a tunnel of thrashing, swirling tree branches. But she hadn't landed on roots. Instead she'd fallen into a dank abyss. The gnarled boughs had swept past her until they blurred, and the sense that she'd fallen for far too long overcame her. That was all she recalled before blacking out.

Waking up here, in this barn, made no sense. Neither did finding four other traumatized women imprisoned with her.

After a week of captivity, Althea had formed and discarded a dozen theories. She was fairly sure they were still in Scotland. The disagreeable odors of sheep and manure had stopped bothering her, but not the cold. The lunatics responsible for this nightmare hadn't given them any blankets or extra clothing. At the moment she could see her breath, but she couldn't feel her nose, ears or fingertips anymore. Soon she'd have to get up and walk around to get warm, but that was only a temporary solution.

If she didn't try to escape and get help, Althea felt convinced they would all die here.

Despite the horrible conditions, she and the other four women taken prisoner had managed to survive well enough. To keep warm during the frigid nights they slept huddled together in the mound of hay by the empty stalls. They'd also managed to get water for drinking and washing from a deep trough well, although it had taken hours to figure out how to work the long pivoting rod to lower and lift their only bucket. Twice a day their guards tossed in some bags containing hard oat cakes and overripe pears, but everyone divided the starvation rations fairly. With the exception of one woman they'd all discussed their situation.

None of them knew what to think about their captors, who were definitely odd and seriously crazy.

The older Scottish couple who seemed to be in charge had talked freely in front of them, so Althea knew all about their delusions. Murdina and Hendry believed they were immortal medieval druids. They believed that she and the other four women were somehow like them, what they called "druid kind," and had the power to allow them to time-travel. They'd been brought to what they claimed was fourteenth century Scotland.

Althea actually had no idea where in Scotland they were. From what she'd seen through the cracks in the barn walls, they'd been brought to a highland forest at the base of a very large mountain. Aside from some white birds, red deer, and a wandering herd of very dirty sheep, the area appeared completely deserted. Althea hadn't seen a single person, car, truck, utility pole or road sign. No aircraft had passed over them in a week. None of their phones could get a signal. The other thing she couldn't explain preyed on her like hungry teeth.

The huge, strange men who had taken all of them might not be human.

"You got any drugs in that thing?" a harsh voice demanded.

Althea looked up at the scowling, dark-haired woman standing over her. Dimly she recalled that her name was Rowan, and that she worked as a carpenter. She'd been taken with her older sister, a lovely, timid dancer who looked and acted nothing like Rowan.

"Drugs?"

"Perrin is sick." She used the toe of her boot to prod Althea's carryall. "You said you were a doctor, right? So, you got aspirin? Ibuprofen? Anything that can help her?"

"I'm sorry, no. I'm not that kind of doctor," she admitted. "Ph.D., not M.D."

"Oh, so you can lecture us while my sister's dying. Fantastic." Rowan made a rude sound indicating the opposite. "We'll call you if someone needs a test graded."

Wishing she really was made of liquid nitrogen, Althea pushed herself to her feet and walked over to where they slept. There Emeline, the black-haired nurse from

Aberdeen, sat pressing a damp rag to the unconscious woman's brow.

She crouched beside her. "Do you know what's making her sick?"

"I've no clue," the nurse said tiredly. She sat back on her heels and took hold of the dancer's wrist. "Her temp and pulse are normal. Her only injuries are the same bruises and lacerations that all of us have. No signs of infection. I simply can't wake her. It could be an allergic reaction—"

Perrin's dark blue eyes snapped open and fixed on Althea's face. Something had made them turn opaque, as if she had gone blind. "Save the raven or we all die." She blinked, and the opacity cleared. "Ro?"

"I think she's back," Emeline said and directed her pen light at Perrin's eyes. "Lass, are you an epileptic? Do you take medication for that or anything else?"

"No and no," Rowan said as she shouldered Althea aside and bent over her sister. "Rise and shine, Big Sis. I swear, you are the laziest chick on the planet." She looked over her shoulder. "Give me your coat."

Althea didn't realize the carpenter was

speaking to her again until she got a dark glare. "Excuse me?"

"She's shivering and sweating, Dr. Useless, so she needs the coat more than you. Unless you've got a blanket stashed in that bag?" She thrust out a pretty hand marred by small scars and calluses. "Come on, hurry up."

The carryall only had a few days change of clothing, and nothing that would fit Perrin. Quickly Althea shrugged out of her coat and handed it to Rowan, who used it to cover Perrin's shaking upper body. Althea felt startled when the fifth prisoner came to stand beside her. An athletic blonde who had stayed curled up in a corner and hadn't yet said a word to anyone, she took off her long white uniform jacket. Leaning down, she draped it over Perrin's long legs and tucked it in like a blanket. Althea recognized the ship emblem embroidered on the jacket's left side. The silent woman worked for a British cruise line.

"Thanks," the carpenter said and stretched out beside her sister and held her as a mother would a sick child. "I've got you, Perr. You're going to be fine."

Emeline gestured Althea to come away

from the sisters and went with her to the other side of the barn. "Don't take that personally. Rowan is just anxious."

"Sure," Althea said. Rowan was aggressive, hostile and terminally snide, and had been since day one. "Some people can't handle being imprisoned, I guess." She noticed the dark circles under the nurse's eyes. "How are you holding up?"

"Like everyone else. Almost feart out of my wits. Also starving, although that's nothing new." She glanced down at her curvaceous figure. "I've been dieting for two months for my best friend's wedding. Which was either yesterday, or not for another seven centuries." She rolled her eyes. "Did I mention this was my first vacation in five years?"

The blonde woman joined them. "Then I won't whinge about hating my first shore leave in six months," she said, croaking out the words as if she were sick, but with a distinctly British accent.

"Hi," Althea said, relieved. She'd been convinced the fifth prisoner had completely lost it. "That was nice, what you did for Perrin."

Emeline nodded her agreement. "Do you have a sore throat?"

"Lost my voice. No," she tacked on when the nurse stepped closer, and cleared her throat with a rasping sound. "It's fine. It's coming back."

Instead of insisting, Emeline nodded and took a step back from the blonde. "Let me know if that changes, ah…"

"Lily Stover. I was a sous-chef on the Atlantia Princess, which is probably halfway to the Bahamas by now." She looked at Althea. "If you want to escape, you'll have to be quick. How fast can you run?"

"When motivated, like the wind," she assured her, and frowned. "How did you know I was—"

"I know the look. Plus, you spend a lot of time in the back stall, where those wood planks have rotted out." The British woman nodded toward the doors as the sound of scraping wood came through them. "Wait until dark. They're slower at night."

The doors flung open as two of the guards came in carrying worn, dirty sacks. Emeline drew Althea and Lily back against the nearest wall, while Rowan shot up and stood between the men and her sister.

Seeing them made Althea feel panicky and sick at the same time. While they appeared to be two towering, heavily-built men, they moved like puppets being jerked by too-loose strings. From a distance no pores, wrinkles or hollows appeared on their faces, giving them a smooth, almost plastic look. Up close an almost imperceptible craquelure webbed their flesh like crazing on old porcelain. All of the guards had cropped hair and wide-set eyes in different shades of brown, but so flat and dull they looked painted.

"Food." The larger of the pair tossed the sack at Rowan's feet, and then eyed Perrin. "Why cover that one? She dead?"

Emeline folded her arms tight around her middle, and Althea knew exactly why. The grating sound of the guard's voice matched that of broken fingernails dragged across splintering wood.

"She's alive," Rowan said and tilted her head back as the guard came to her, but otherwise didn't move. "We covered her because she's freezing, genius."

"We're all pure cold," Emeline said quickly. "If we could have some blankets—"

"Use the grass," the guard said and bent his head to peer into Rowan's dark eyes. His thin lips peeled back from his yellowed tombstone teeth. "If I want the skinny one, I shall take her. You cannae stop me."

"You don't want her. She won't fight you." The dark woman leaned in closer. "But I will. Come on. Give me a try, Ugly."

The guard made as if to grab her, but the other one dragged him back.

"Go, Coig," he said as he thrust the bigger man toward the doors. He shoved the sack he held into Rowan's hands and waited until the other guard left. "Dinnae challenge us. You shallnae survive it."

"You mean if we're nice to you, we live?" Rowan said and uttered a short laugh. "Right. Kill me now, Shorty."

"You call me Ochd." The guard started to reach for her himself, and then backed away. He bobbled his head around to look at Althea and the other women. "Eat. Sleep. Make trouble, and Coig comes back. Coig likes hurting." He nodded at Lily. "She ken."

Althea swallowed some bile as Ochd went out and slammed the barn doors shut. "Lily, what did he mean?"

"That bloody bastard, Coig, took me from the market where I was shopping. He lugged me out by my neck." The blonde tugged down the high collar of her shirt to show the huge, dark bruises mottling her slim throat. "And he bashed in the skull of a farmer who tried to stop him." She met Althea's gaze. "With one fist."

Chapter Five

❧❧❧

CADEYRN KEPT PACE with Brennus's longer strides as they led the clan to the river. "The old man may be lying about these powers."

"Aye, for his lips moved," Brennus said. He stopped at the edge of the bank and regarded the depth of the rushing currents. "Shaman, reckon."

Clansmen shifted aside as Ruadri, the largest warrior among them, came from his retral position to join the chieftain. While a head taller and an arm's reach wider than most of his brothers, Ruadri moved sound-lessly, and with a sinuous ease that always unnerved their enemies. The sun on his blue-sheened black hair made the wide silver streaks at his temples look as if spell light poured from them. His prodigious size made his garments strain at the seams. His battle spirit skinwork, half-moons inked on his outer forearms, glowed faintly as he glanced back at Bhaltair.

"Our indenture brands have gone," Ruadri said, his cavernous voice carrying so that every man touched their now-smooth napes. "My ward marks, Kanyth's burns and Cadeyrn's lash scars as well. Only transformation magic could scour them from our hides." Old hatred blackened his gray eyes. "The tree-knower likely doesnae deceive us on that."

Brennus nodded. "I shall lead. If 'tis truth, and I change, you and the clan follow me to Dun Mor."

"And if it doesnae?" Cadeyrn asked, looking skeptical.

"Then we'll have a bathe before our long walk." He checked the depths again before wading into the water up to his hips.

As the currents buffeted him, Brennus kept his footing and let the water flow around his hands and legs. At first the river merely felt icy and wet, and then he felt something go liquid in his core. When he looked down he saw his form paling, as if he were fading away, and lifted his hand to his face. His long fingers now looked as if they'd been turned to blue-tinted glass, and an odd satisfaction filled him.

Imagining the stream that spiraled around Dun Mor, the Skaraven's secret highland stronghold, Brennus dove into the currents.

Magic poured out of his now-transparent form, and the water around him churned with huge bubbles of light. Colors and shapes flashed around him as his body shot through the river, streaming through it a thousand times faster than on a charging warhorse.

The transformation magic had not changed him into water. It had made him brother to it.

His jaunt slowed and then stopped in colder, darker currents, where Brennus found his footing. As he surfaced his body solidified and broke through a thin layer of ice.

Snow drifted down on his shoulders and head as he climbed out of the frozen stream. Shedding cascades from his saturated garments onto the steep, rocky bank, he made his way to a wide mound of stone and jumped up to survey his surroundings.

Frost-edged wind swirled around Brennus as he took in the woodlands. No villages or towns had intruded on the remote massif, which seemed to have grown bigger and wilder since last the Skaraven had left. Narrow tracks, too small to belong to humans, stitched their way through the drifts. He filled his lungs with the cold highland air, which tasted of snow and sky, before he leapt down and returned to the river's edge.

The currents roiled with light and froth as Cadeyrn rose, his grim expression disappearing as he looked down at himself and then at Brennus. "Skelp me, Bren."

Hearing his second call him by his boyhood name almost made him smile. "Bring your face here, then, Cade."

The War Master winced. "I'd rather no' nurse the first jaw you shatter." His gaze shifted around them. "Gods above, 'tis truly the Great Wood."

Seeing his clan emerge from the water dispelled most of Brennus's ire. The ability to travel in this manner would give the Skaraven many advantages. It might even be possible for them to cross a sea without a vessel. He felt a quiet pride in his men as the first waded out of the stream and took defensive positions on either side. They may have been dead for twelve centuries, and bewildered by these new abilities, but their loyalty to the clan remained absolute and unwavering.

Ruadri, the last to emerge, dropped down on the bank and he spread his arms. The rest of the clan took to one knee while Brennus kept watch.

"Battle spirits above and within, we dinnae ask your notice, yet you see," the big man said. "Watch now over us as we fight to live free. By the Gods' will, so shall we be."

"So shall we be," the clan echoed as one, and then struck the ground with their fists and rose.

Brennus went to his shaman, hoisting him up from the ground. "Will they follow, do you reckon?"

Ruadri shook his head. "Flen led them away before I entered the river, Chieftain. The pact of indenture died with the two tribes.

These druids ken that they hold no power over us."

Bitterness soured his words, reminding Brennus how much it gnawed at his shaman to have dealings with the tree-knowers. He reached out to the other man. "You've only our souls to manage now, Ru."

"Aye, Bren." He clasped the chieftain's forearm and touched their shoulders. "Glad I'm of it."

"If you two doves have finished billing and cooing," a mellow voice said, "we should see to the keepe."

Brennus turned to look into eyes that mirrored his own. All of the Skaraven considered themselves brothers, but he and Kanyth shared kinship through the same sire. Just as tall but far more handsome, his half-brother had long arms and a wide, massive upper torso built by a lifetime of serving his forge battle spirit. "I see twelve centuries in the earth hasnae tamed your tongue, Weapons Master."

"Aye, Chieftain, but I'm much prettier now." Kanyth spread his huge hands, now absent the layers of burn scars that had before mottled his flesh. "No' that I wish to squeeze your spleen, but if the keepe remains, we'll yet need to fetch food, water and wood." He swatted at the streaming locks of bronze hair framing his angular face. "And shears, before this clan begins bleating for a barn."

Brennus watched as grins and chuckles spread through his clan. Ever practical, his younger brother also knew how to quickly dispel tensions. Not for the first time did he wonder if Kanyth would have served better as their chieftain.

"Ruadri and Cadeyrn with me to the keepe." To his brother he said, "Send scouts to check the trails and boundaries. Set vine snares and collect straight wood to fashion spears. Remain unseen. We'll signal when 'tis clear."

Time had erased most of their old paths through the Great Wood, but Brennus had trained himself and the clan to find their way to Dun Mor in the dark. As he led his second and the shaman through the dense brush, he noted the other changes twelve centuries had wrought on their land. The surrounding hills and mountains had further eroded into smooth waves of granite and snow, while new groves of pines, birch and alder had spread through the rims of the valley. Snow devils still danced along the edges of the ridges and deep cirques, but the white drifts that rarely melted seemed much wider and deeper.

Brennus stopped at the labyrinth of what appeared to be weathered tors at the base of an enormous rockfall swathing one slope of the plateau. Heavy carpets of moss and lichen splotched the ancient stones, and deep piles of rotted leaves, snapped twigs and pebbles mounded at their bases. To see the stones weathered by time but still joined as the clan had built them made him feel a flicker of hope.

Cadeyrn handed him a broken pine branch wrapped at one end with a swath of dry, dead moss, and fashioned two more for himself and Ruadri. "I left my firebox on the hall mantle."

"Never could you put away a thing proper." He held up his hand, aligning his thumb and forefinger with the center tor, and took two paces to the left before he walked directly into the granite.

What appeared to be stone from without remained an illusion created by the positioning of the worn stone pillars. Brennus's shoulders brushed their sides as he entered the maze leading into the Skaraven stronghold. It had taken the clan two seasons to quarry and haul the stones to conceal the entrance to their keepe, and here they were, waiting like old friends to welcome them.

Deep within the maze, he stopped at a tightly-jointed wedge of rock, and pushed at the left corner of the top stone. For a long moment nothing happened, and then a scraping sound grated in the air. The right half of the granite slowly swung out on its weighted pivot to reveal a tall, wide doorway in the stone.

"Shaman," Brennus said, "regard."

Ruadri joined him, and lifted his hands. The half-moons on his arms glittered with a surge of his power as he closed his eyes. A moment later he dropped his hands and nodded to Brennus. "Naught within."

Stepping through the doorway, Brennus entered the long hall they had hewn through the fallen rock. As he expected, the air in the keepe's

dark interior smelled stale and musty. When his
boots crushed the rotted floor rushes, small
clouds of murky dust rose around them. He
made his way by memory to the huge center
hearth and felt along the mantle. There he found
a carved box covered in dust. From it he took a
firesteel and flint, and used them to light the dry
moss on the branch. Once a flame flared, he
touched the end to the branches his men held,
and the torches lit up their surroundings.

Curtains of old spiderwebs undulated
overhead as Brennus turned slowly to take in
the Skaraven's hall. Rock dust thickly covered
every surface, from the cracked mantle over
the big stone hearth to the collapsed long,
wooden tables and benches where the clan
had once gathered for their meals. The fine
tapestries that had adorned their stone walls
had fallen into heaps of rotted debris. The
great wooden raven still hung mounted above
the stone staircase leading down to the lower
levels of the stronghold, but time had turned it
as black as their clan rings.

"Fack me," Cadeyrn muttered. "'Tis
become a tomb."

Not quite, but it would take weeks to restore order, Brennus thought. He picked up a rusted iron rod from beside the mantle and said, "Cade, open the air shaft doors, and check the treasury. Ru, tend to the hearth. I'll go below."

Using the iron to clear the webs lacing the passage leading down into the tunnels, Brennus felt the stillness of the subterranean level wash over him. He and the clan had built Dun Mor to endure as they had. It had withstood the highland's ever-changeable weather, harsh winters, and the weight of twelve centuries. He should have felt gratified that their efforts had proven sound, and yet his mind traveled back to the moment he'd awoken. In his memory he saw those wide, crystalline blue eyes, and heard that terrified, cut-off scream.

He'd never been plagued by visions, as Ruadri often was, but he'd had his share of evil dreams. Yet everything about the lass had seemed so real. Even if she was not a trick of his mind, he knew her fate. The giants never let live the mortals they took. He could only

hope they had not first tortured that strange,
beautiful lady.

Thinking of her turned his mood dark, so
that when he reached his private chambers he
wrenched the old door off its hinges. Torchlight revealed what he had expected inside: his
furnishings rotted and his weapons rusted.
Mold encased his trunk, eating through the
wood to devour his garments. The shelf of
maps and scrolls he'd collected in life now held
only small mounds of insect-riddled fragments. Water had dripped down from a crack
in the ceiling stone and collected in a pool that
now lay frozen over the blackened depression
formed by countless other thaws.

The Skaraven had never coveted posses-
sions, as few had been permitted. To see what
little he'd had stolen from him by time,
however, made new fury bloom inside him.

Ruinous as their lives had been, was
nothing left of them?

Brennus backed out of the chamber to
seek the one room where he could vent his
frustrations. A narrow shadow crossed his, and
he impatiently regarded the man waiting for
him. Appearing thin compared to most of the

Skaraven, Taran had a taut, sinewy build like the swiftest of stallions, and a mane of white-blond hair that he'd already woven into a long braid.

He saw himself in the clansman's lochan-blue eyes, and rammed back his roiling emotions. "What do you here, Horse Master?"

Taran shrugged.

Brennus knew why he had come. When other men spoke Taran watched and listened. While he preferred to be among his beasts, he had an uncanny sense when one of the men needed to unburden himself. Since their boyhood he had never repeated such confidences, even when beaten by their trainers. No one spoke of it, but all Skaraven trusted the Horse Master as the clan's keeper of secrets.

"'Tis all we had, and now gone," the chieftain found himself admitting. "We've no' so much as a dagger between us."

"As 'twas when first we came here, Bren, and no' all dust." Taran reached out to touch the tunnel wall as if stroking the flank of a favored mare. "We persist as does Dun Mor's stone. 'Tis still standing, and 'tis ours. 'Tis home."

"Aye, and we live again, and flash through water like graylings gone mad, and the Gods ken what more." He frowned as the face of the flame-haired lass came into his thoughts. "Tran, if we are to break the old chains, we must leave Caledonia for Gaul, or Hispania, or another land free of the magic folk. 'Tis what I must do to protect our brothers."

"Yet 'tis no' what you wish to do." The horse master tapped the side of his head. "Think again on it. Speak with the clan. Then choose." His mouth hitched. "We've followed you to our deaths. To Gaul seems a garden stroll."

Brennus accompanied Taran upstairs, where Cadeyrn had the hearth and dozens of torches lit. Men marched in and out as they cleared the detritus from the hall. For a moment he stood and watched his brothers working together to make habitable the old stronghold. They had already begun to put behind them the shock of this stunning awakening.

"We persist," Taran murmured before he headed to help a pair of clansmen wrestling to shore up some cracked support timbers.

Kanyth entered with a group of their best hunters, each carrying snares of game and greenwood. They'd use the wood to make spears and build a new spit for the hearth. Ruadri had uncapped the stronghold's interior well, and knelt beside it as he carefully drew out a stone cask brimming with water. Judging by his expression when he sampled it, their supply had remained unspoiled.

"Weapons Master," Brennus called. "Scout the forge."

His half-brother eyed his hands and heaved a sigh before he called back, "Aye, Chieftain" and trudged off.

Cadeyrn came to report. "No new settlements within our boundaries or beyond them. The pit traps are filled to the brim with leaves and rot, but some of our blinds remain. We sighted vast herds of reindeer, elk, red deer—no' white, thank the Gods—and mountain sheep, all fat and shaggy for winter." He held up a hastily-made purse. "Our coffers remain untouched."

They had fire, water, game to hunt for food, and shelter. The clan's treasury had been bursting with gold and silver from hiring out as mercenaries during the few years of freedom they'd had. Brennus would have preferred to hear the men had also found a cache of two hundred newly-forged blades, but it would do until Kanyth could fashion more.

"Take nine men by water to Aberdeen. Buy only what is necessary for the keepe, and that you may carry back with you. And Cade," he added as the War Master turned away. "Say naught of the clan."

"Aye, and me as eager as a lad to tell tales of digging out of our graves with our baws swinging in the breeze." His expression turned rueful. "While my tongue might flap as hard, we've no' forgotten ourselves, Chieftain."

"I saw that at the river, Brother." He clapped his second's shoulder. "Safe journey."

To make Dun Mor temporarily habitable Brennus issued orders for the stewards to clear the floors and mound dry moss and leaves in the hall for beds. He set his best hunters and masons to work together to fashion enough spears for five patrols this night, and then bowls and cups for the clan's meals. The rest of the clan he put to salvage what could still be used from the stronghold's myriad stores. Once the men had their orders, Brennus caught their shaman's eye and beckoned to him.

"The keep's water yet runs clear and sweet," Ruadri told him. "'Tis warm enough for a wash."

"The flow must have found its way to the hot spring." He saw the shaman's expression and recalled how much Ruadri had favored a steaming bath. "You'll have your soak soon enough. Walk with me."

Ruadri accompanied the chieftain outside, to find guards already positioned to defend the keepe. Each held spears and stone slings made from patches cut from their boots.

"Keep watchful," he told the men, who acknowledged the command by tapping their clan rings against the spear shafts.

Ruadri remained silent until they reached the stream. "My soak can wait. I'll go with you."

"You'll stay and attend to the clan. Some of our brothers sorely need your counsel." He nodded toward the west. "I'll visit the moun-

tain and see how many giants returned.
'Tis all."

"If they've among them a female healer…" Ruadri said and shook his head.

Brennus thought of his own flame-haired
vision. "Tell me the rest."

"I cannae tell you what 'twas, only that I
saw her before we rose. Young, snow-skinned
and black-haired, with blue eyes like the tribe
of Ara." The shaman's voice grew flinty. "The
famhair dragged her from an iron cart of a
kind I didnae ken, and then into the ground."
He rubbed his brow. "I dinnae ken why I
speak of it. If 'twas real, the giants have
killed her."

It seemed the Gods had toyed with Ruadri
as well.

"I'll look. If I dinnae return by tomorrow
dawn, name Cadeyrn chieftain, prepare the
clan for travel, and go." Before the shaman
could reply Brennus waded out into the
stream to let his flesh bond with the water
before he submerged.

A few moments later he surfaced from the
dark waters of a lochan near the base of
Beinn Nibheis, startling a mass of sheep

grazing in the adjoining glen. They hurried across the fields and into the trees. More than the scent of the herd tainted the air, and he followed the stink of rot to the battered body of an old shepherd. The man's skewed head and distorted limbs made it plain that his bones had been snapped like twigs. His flesh showed no sign that he had been beaten. But his face still wore terror like a frozen mask— the kind that the sight of giants might make.

Too many times had Brennus seen the same among those killed by the *famhairean*.

He eyed the forest. In the past the giants had always encamped in huge, remote woods where their druid conspirators could use their forest magic. They would kill any mortal who crossed their path. Doubtless the dead shepherd had done so. Brennus knew at this hour the giants had the power of the sun to aid them, and to brace them alone would be foolhardy. He'd find a spot to conceal himself and wait for nightfall, and then enter the forest and begin his search.

As he walked toward a cluster of large boulders by the water he spotted something bright in the grass. He scooped up the broken

silver chain, and held it up to inspect the glittering crystal heart hanging from it. In his
memory its twin sparkled around the neck of
the flame-haired lass a moment before she had
been taken. Now a dark smear marred the
cracked gem, which split in two on his palm.

I shall avenge you, my lady. Tightly he
clenched his fist over the shards.

He felt the tiny thrum against his palm,
and opened his fingers to stare at the intact
crystal, from which the dried blood had disappeared. He had no magic, so whatever
enchanted it had to be hers. Feeling the delicate beat on his skin filled him with inexplicable, savage joy.

They'd brought her here and she was still
alive.

Chapter Six

ALTHEA WAITED UNTIL Perrin had gotten up before she retrieved her jacket and shrugged into it. Her share of the evening food went into her zippered pockets, and she braided her dirty hair back from her face, tying it with a loose string from her torn shirt. Checking the stall where she'd used a piece of old hemp sacking to cover a mound of hay she'd shaped to look like a body, she looped the braided cord through her jeans, tying it in a knot. She thrust her arms through the carryall's handles so she could wear it like a backpack, and then looked over at Emeline, who was watching her from the front of the barn.

Okay, Rowan, she thought as she retreated

to the back stall. *Now you just have to be the obnox-ious bitch we've all come to know and avoid.*

"Hey, Rowan," the nurse said, "can you draw some water for me? These pears need a wash, and my shoulder is still giving me grief."

Lily had been the one to suggest sabo-taging the frame supporting the well pole as a distraction. The sous-chef pointed out that they could make it fall over by discreetly removing some of the stones piled around the base. Emeline had agreed, arguing that if the fall broke the frame apart, they could easily build another one using some of the wood from the stalls.

"When she finds out we deliberately did this, Rowan will be pissed," Althea told the other woman once they'd quietly discussed the plan.

Emeline looked worried. "We should tell her what we're doing. She'll help. I know she will."

"It works better if she doesn't know," Lily said. "And what will she do? Never speak to us again? That would be ruddy brilliant." She made a dismissive gesture. "Just be ready."

The one thing the three of them agreed

on was that Perrin wouldn't survive an escape attempt. Emeline wasn't convinced she'd survive at all and felt compelled to stay and help care for her. Lily had never said she'd stay in so many words, but Althea had sensed it. After what the woman had been through with Coig, she could hardly be blamed.

Althea waited until the sound of the frame crashing and Rowan erupting angrily filled the air, and then pushed out two of the stall's rotted planks. As she watched through the hole she'd created, the guard posted at the back of the barn trudged around to the front. She had to wriggle to get through the narrow gap, but as soon as she emerged outside she ran.

Go, go, and don't look back.

Withered shrubs and frosty tree branches clawed at Althea as she hurried into the dark forest. She deliberately avoided the sheep trails leading away from the homestead and ran in the opposite direction. She didn't dare slow down or look back over her shoulder until she emerged from the trees and saw the moonlight gleaming on a small lake surrounded by boulders. Althea saw her breath puffing out in white clouds in front of her, but no sign of other people, houses, roads or any form of civilization. The moonlight silvered a lovely but empty vista of hills and woods and tinier lakes as far as she could see.

This couldn't be. The rock mounds by the lake blocked her view of part of the land beyond. She wove her way through the trees as she tried to find a better vantage spot.

Brush rustled as two of the guards came out of the woods on her left. She held her breath and pressed against a broad trunk as she watched them walk down to the lake. They stopped a few yards away from the water and glanced back directly at her.

A deep shout shattered the air, and a huge dark shape, like some enormous black bird, soared out of the boulders.

One of the guards jumped up, colliding with what Althea could now see was a man with black hair as long as a cape, which had made him looked winged. They both fell to the ground, and the second guard jumped on top of the pair. Both guards began pounding the pinned man with their fists.

Save the raven, or we all die.

Perrin's eerie demand roared in Althea's head, and then she couldn't think anymore. She shoved herself away from the trunk and ran to them. She knew she was running to her death, but if it gave the dark man time to escape, then it might save the lives of the other women.

He had to live too.

As soon as Althea reached the men she flung her hands out to shove the bigger guard away. The moment she touched him something flashed through her, as cutting and cold as a blade made of ice. All the warmth in her body suddenly dissipated as the air grew thick, and a sound like distant, shattering glass crackled in her ears.

She felt as if she were freezing, but why? Who was doing this to her? The dark man?

The guard's face turned white and stiff. A wave of thick frost crept up and formed a flat mask over his face. Then it raced down his bull neck and over his shoulders. As it covered him he fell off the dark man, his limbs still frozen in place as he landed on his back. One of his arms broke off and fell beside him.

"Druid whore," the other guard muttered as

he grabbed Althea by the throat and jerked her off her feet.

Althea hung dangling from his stranglehold, and darkness filled her eyes. The freezing cold intensified around them and when the guard's fist turned white with ice, he dropped her. She fell shivering and coughing to the ground as the frozen guard toppled over onto his comrade.

The dark man appeared over them with a huge rock in his hands. With giant, pummeling blows, he smashed it down on the pair. Ice flew, pelting Althea, as he crushed the guards into a pile of splintered wood and slush. Though she tried to crawl away, the dark man seized her and lifted her onto her feet. He looked all over her as if he couldn't believe she was there.

God, he was real. "Who are you?" she whispered.

Before he could answer two blindingly-bright lights rose from the remains of the guards. Althea squinted to watch them fly over her head and smash into two pines at the edge of the woods.

She couldn't stop shaking even as the dark

man pressed something into her numb fingers. When she staggered away, he didn't try to grab her. Althea glanced down to see her necklace in her hand, and then stared at him.

Was he part of this? Would he turn her to ice and smash her to bits?

She turned and stumbled toward the woods, but fell over something erupting from the soil. She screamed as two huge, slithering roots enveloped her boots and legs and dragged her toward the pine trees that now glowed. The roots grew tighter and, as they did, they ripped through her jeans and bit into her flesh.

The dark man put himself between her and the woods. His massive hands gripped the roots and tore them apart before he hoisted her into his arms and ran toward the lake. Althea's vision darkened as she felt blood welling from her legs and the coldness solidifying in her torso. Desperately she focused on the dark man, who had stopped at the edge of the water and was pulling her closer.

"The others," she managed to get out through her chattering teeth. "Save them, please."

His black eyes narrowed, and then he bent his head and covered her mouth with his. As more roots slithered toward them he dove into the lake.

Bubbling light surrounded Althea, who couldn't breathe anymore. All she felt was the dark man's hard, hungry mouth on hers, and then nothing as she lost consciousness.

Chapter Seven

I N THE SUBTERRANEAN level of Dun Mor, Brennus stood at the back of Ruadri's healing chamber and watched as the shaman used a new blade to cut away the lass's shredded trews. He'd already applied woundwort and yarrow to the wounds he had exposed. Brennus's gut knotted as he took in all of the ugly gashes slashing across her delicate skin. To see her like this made him want to return to the mountain with the clan and kill everything that moved.

"'Tis no' so bad," Ruadri said, his voice low and soft. "She's chilled, but that slowed the bleeding. She'll be hobbled for a time, but I reckon 'twill all mend."

Brennus pushed some of the damp hair

away from the swelling gash on the side of her head. "And the blow she took here?"

"I'll ken more of that when she wakes. Better there than the back of her neck. That 'twould have ended her." The shaman regarded him. "When you carried her in, Bren, you said she saved you. How did you mean, saved?"

"Just so. I crossed the path of two *famhairean*, and they attacked me." Brennus let the delicate strands of her hair sift through his fingers before he stepped back. "Both had me pinned when she came from the forest and turned them to ice. Froze them to their cores with but a touch of her hands."

"Did she utter a spell before she touched them?" When Brennus shook his head Ruadri rubbed the back of his broad neck. "'Tis no' a tree-knower's gift. Did you see the black-haired healer?"

"Only this lass, and I've never seen the like of what she did. Once the giants fell from me I broke them apart like riddled kindling. They discarded their remains and used two more trees to attack her." He nodded at her legs. "Their roots did that when they seized her."

"So the giants still can use other trees, but cannae die. Our luck remains dismal." The shaman covered her with a fleece before he went over to toss more wood on the chamber's hearth. "I gave her a potion for the pain. 'Twill keep her asleep for the night. Now you should go and attend to the clan."

Brennus frowned. "What of the men?"

"They ken that you've brought a young, beautiful woman to Dun Mor. Some saw her and her strange garments. She's no' from our land. I cannae open that satchel she had strapped to her back." Ruadri glanced at the unconscious female. "To have her here among us, even for me to treat her wounds, 'twould never have been permitted."

"Before we rose, no," Brennus told him. "We shall live as all men do now."

The shaman's expression grew thoughtful. "But after so long, can we?"

"If I've to beat the freedom into your heads, aye, we will." He strode out of the chamber and mounted the stairs up to the keepe level, where most of the clan had gathered around the hearth. They collectively turned to look at him, their expressions guarded but their eyes filled with strong emotions.

"War, Weapons, Horse, counsel in my chambers. Bring the lass's satchel." Brennus deliberately let his gaze sweep around the room. "The rest of you, find a bed and sleep. We shall speak of this and other matters on the morrow."

The men reluctantly scattered while Brennus led his advisors below ground. While he had been at the mountain the clan had repaired his door and done much to make his chamber more habitable. The old decayed furnishings had been removed, and in their place stood a new bed draped with blue silk over a generous pile of snowy fleece. Fine curtains and tapestries covered the stained walls, and a thick rug stretched out under a big, grand-looking hide chair by the hearth.

"We couldnae buy much made garb, but we found a tailor willing to send for more. He'll clothe the clan within sevenday. An obliging herd of sheep in the next valley provided bedding," Cadeyrn said as he watched the chieftain inspect the room.

"Kanyth fashioned shears from what iron could be salvaged."

"I've a mountain of rust in the forge's upper stores," the weapons master admitted. "But the ore in the undercroft remains intact and dry. 'Tis enough to fashion ten thousand blades."

"We want but a hundred," Brennus said. He knew the pain his half-brother would suffer while making weapons for the men, for his power over iron came with a price. "Dinnae burn yourself to the bone in the making, Ka."

His men listened without comment as Brennus related what had happened when he'd been attacked at the lochan. Once he finished, Cadeyrn began to scowl and pace. Kanyth grinned and Taran looked alarmed.

"I cannae think of what to do with the lady," Brennus said, prompting his second to stop and give him an incredulous look. "Dinnae be crass, Cade. She's no' a pleasure lass. Nor shall I permit her to be treated as one."

"'Tis the only manner of wench we've ever ken," Cadeyrn reminded him as he picked up the satchel and studied the long, odd-looking seam at the top. He pulled a tiny metal tab, and the seam parted with a slithering sound. He tugged it in the opposite direction, and the seam closed again. "What do you make of that? 'Tis unnatural."

"'Tis a fastener," Brennus said, keeping a straight face. "Mayhap she'll teach you to make such."

"So comes true my dream to be apprenticed to a satchel-maker." Cadeyrn sighed. "She's a tree-knower, Bren. I say we hand her back to her people. She's their burden, no' ours."

"I say no'," Kanyth put in. "She did save you, Chieftain, and 'tis no' a debt to be repaid with words."

Brennus regarded his half-brother. "What do you reckon as fitting?"

"To abide here in safety with the Skaraven." He folded his big hands behind his back. "This ice magic she possesses to vanquish the *famhairean*, 'twould be useful to us. As mine has been, and mayhap more so. She could teach Ruadri the magic she wields. He's clever and strong enough to resist her beauty. She mentioned others. We may go take them from the giants and learn if they have similar gifts."

"You dinnae ken what she is," Taran said suddenly. "Flen said the giants came back from the future. Mayhap they stole her from that time. If 'tis so, we should strive to return her."

Brennus thought all their advice had some weight to it, but he could not see himself handing the lass over to the druids. Nor could he use her for her magic. Even if it could somehow be managed, the prospect of returning her to a distant future made him feel as if he contemplated cutting off an arm or leg.

Why she seemed so important to him remained a mystery. Nor could he fathom how he would ever repay her for the life-debt. Until he understood the first and resolved the second, he'd keep the lady safe.

"She's too hurt to travel," he finally told his men. "She'll stay below for now. I'll watch over her while I think on it."

His second nodded and left, and after a long, troubled look Taran did the same. That left him alone with his half-brother, who waited with his arms folded, and one brow raised.

"Dinnae prod me, Ka," Brennus told him. "Else you want your face less comely."

Kanyth's roofbeam shoulders rolled. "Use it if you wish. I'll heal by morn." He winked. "And I'll always be prettier than you."

"Before Flen's awakening, I had a vision of the lady," he found himself admitting. "She knelt in the forest, gathering ferns."

"A pretty fancy, but that isnae what troubles you." His brother eyed the satchel. "What of her, then?"

"I saw her face again tonight, when she ran to save me," Brennus admitted. "'Twas plain, the fear she felt. She ken that she would likely die in the effort, and yet she ran to me still. What manner of lass does such?"

"One who'd rather fight than cower, which doesnae to me seem like mortal or druid kind." Kanyth spread his newly-scarred hands. "Mayhap she's a goddess."

Chapter Eight

❧❧❧

I N A GOLDEN darkness, Althea held
onto the dark man kissing her. Pushing
him away seemed unlikely, and for some
reason she couldn't breathe through her nose.
Then he breathed for her through their
mouths, filling her lungs. He kept doing that
instead of kissing her, and she felt his body
move against her. His chest felt like a wave did
at the edge of the ocean, when it surged
around someone standing in the sand.

She liked breathing this way. He could
breathe for her forever.

As the sky turned from gilded onyx to
emerald, Althea felt long, silky feathers tickling
her cold fingers. She opened her eyes and saw
them, strewn through the blue glass curtain of

his hair. The hair and feathers slowly turned black, which puzzled her. How could he change his coloring so fast? Why did the feathers look completely natural, as if they were growing out of his scalp?

No wonder they were flying. The man really was part raven.

She marveled at her own calm, but then her fears had dissolved completely. Had she ever felt this safe? Probably not since her uncle had passed away. They broke through something, and she became aware of the rain pouring over them. He lifted his mouth from hers, and water beaded the thick lashes around his black eyes. She'd seen those eyes before this moment, even before the fight with the guards.

He'd tried to save her in the forest.

Althea recalled the moment before she'd been taken, when she'd looked up to see a shadow of a man reaching for her. At first all she'd seen of his face were his beautiful dark eyes filled with some inexplicable rage. Then the rest of his features appeared, savagely handsome and not angry at all, but as baffled as she'd felt. Then his gaze had shifted, and he'd shouted something soundlessly.

She'd read the words on his lips: *Behind you.*

The dark man had tried to warn her, had tried to save her, but when he touched her his hands had passed through her like a ghost's. None of it had happened. Afterward, sitting in the barn with the other women, Althea decided the whole thing had been a fear-induced hallucination. He hadn't been real. In a moment of extreme terror she'd imagined him.

Only her imaginary man now waded out of the water, carrying her past huge piles of stone and up a steep slope. The night crowded in on her cold, shivering body, and Althea felt so tired she gratefully sank into a blissfully empty void.

Waking a second time came with the sensation of cool, dry air on her throbbing legs, and the feeling of motion. Althea became aware of the big, hard arms cradling her battered body from beneath as she was carried. She could feel the slow, heavy thud of a heartbeat under her cheek. From the feel of the material on her skin she guessed someone had wrapped her legs with soft, damp bandages before dressing her in a long top. Her back hurt, and a bittersweet taste lingered in her mouth.

She shifted her head down before she opened her eyes to mere slits.

A very large, well-built man was carrying her through a passage with rough stone walls. From the wild mane of black hair hanging over his shoulders he had to be the dark man from her dream, minus the feathers.

Where was he taking her, and why? This couldn't be a hospital or police station.

As the dark man stopped to open a door Althea forced herself to remain limp and unresisting. As long as he thought she was still unconscious she had the upper hand. She couldn't see much as he carried her into the room and over to a bed or table covered with sheep's wool. There he lowered her onto her side and draped her with a cloud of something clinging and soft, like fine silk.

She nearly flinched when she heard the sound of metal clanking, and dared to take another peek. Cloaked by the fall of his hair, the dark man snapped two crude-looking shackles around her ankles before he straightened and looked down at her.

Althea closed her eyes, hoping he hadn't seen her watching. The restraints scared her almost as much as he did. Why was he shackling her to the bed? Had she gone through hell just to trade one prison for another? The pain in her back and the bandages winding around her legs reminded her of those last moments, when he'd torn apart the roots dragging her into the woods.

No, he wouldn't hurt me. He saved my life.

She felt the warmth of his hand a moment before he touched her cheek. He didn't stroke her or do anything but let his fingertips rest against her skin. The touch sent heat spreading over her face, as if he'd set fire to her nerves. She swallowed a gasp and kept concentrating on taking deep, slow breaths.

His scent washed over her, warm and male and intensely alluring. Comforting, too, in a way she'd never before felt. For a moment Althea thought she might fling herself into his arms.

He withdrew his hand, and his heavy footsteps moved away from her. She waited until she heard the door creak shut before she peeked again. When she felt sure he'd left her alone, she opened her eyes.

She propped herself up on her elbow to get a better look at the room. Carved out of solid rock, it seemed more like a giant cave. The bed, which from the fractures in the wood appeared to have been recently repaired, would have been more at home in a museum. Several intricately hand-made tapestries hung from spikes hammered into the stone walls, each depicting nature scenes with simple yet artful stitching. So either he liked medieval reproductions or she really was in fourteenth-century Scotland.

"Or under it," Althea muttered, wincing as she sat up.

Pulling the blue silk coverlet away, she glanced down and bit her lower lip. The long top she wore looked like a crudely-made wool tunic. Under it she was naked, but that didn't worry her as much as the wounds.

The bizarre root attack had really done a number on her legs. Loosely-woven linen strips wound around each from ankle to upper thigh. She couldn't see her back, but the throbbing told her she had some significant wounds back there. Easing away the edges of her leg bandages, she found multiple gashes of various depths and lengths laddering each limb.

"Trees did this," she murmured, appalled.

She knew lateral root systems often proved to be stronger than those closest to the tree. They acted as its anchor to prevent it from toppling over in a strong wind. But these roots had behaved as if they were sapient. She knew certain types of bamboo could grow up to thirty-five inches in a day, but these roots had elongated fifty yards in seconds. If the dark man hadn't torn them apart, they might have done the same to her. Althea had no clue as to how they had grown so fast or behaved like tentacles, but if it was the last thing she ever did, she'd find out.

The dark man or whoever had treated her injuries had also applied an herbal poultice that had dried over the wounds, sealing them like a natural bandage. When she pinched a fragment of the concoction and held it to her nose, she smelled the chrysanthemum-like scent of yarrow. Closer inspection helped her identify the spiky remains of self-heal flowers. She knew both to be excellent herbal treatments for staunching bleeding.

The dark man or his doctor knew their plants. Maybe they'd done this to continue the ruse to convince her she had landed in the fourteenth century. Maybe this was all part of the lunatics' scheme.

The door opened, making Althea flinch, but she had no time to play possum again. The dark man came in carrying a tray with a silver goblet and a steaming bowl. He stopped in his tracks as he saw her sitting up, and then slowly approached.

Seeing him clearly for the first time made her feel dizzy. Almost seven feet tall, the dark man had a heavily-muscled frame and long, strong-looking limbs. He wore a shabby tunic over new trousers, both made of dark, dense wool, and boots made of hide-side-out fur. On his right hand he wore a black ring carved to resemble a bird looking over its shoulder. His thick black hair hung down around his hips, where it caught the light from the fireplace and gleamed sapphire and violet.

He kept his gaze locked with hers but didn't say a word.

As he came closer Althea gave into a surge of panic and painfully pushed herself back to put as much space between them as she could. She only relaxed a little when she saw that his face didn't have the weird crackling like the things that had taken her. She watched as he placed the tray on the side of the bed, and then retreated to the big chair on the other side of the room. There he sat by the hearth and watched her in return.

She'd saved his life, and he'd saved hers. So why was he keeping her prisoner?

Althea glanced away long enough to see what he'd brought. The goblet appeared to be filled with water, while the bowl held a mound of steaming oatmeal topped with dark purple berries. Her empty stomach rumbled miserably, but she didn't go near the tray. If he meant to drug her, he'd have to shove the pills down her throat.

No, this isn't about hurting me. He could have done that while I was unconscious. He could be doing that right now.

She felt overwhelmed by the confusion of

images from what she last remembered of this man. The memory of him soaring through the air in the shape of an enormous raven should have terrified her, not filled her with wonder. The guards coming out of the woods had seen her, but went first to attack him. Was that why he'd jumped into the air like that? As a diversion?

Did he save my life first?

The rest became muddled with the cold, the terror, and her pain. But the one thing she remembered was the first guard freezing. The moment she'd touched him something cold had flashed through her, and all the warmth had left her body.

Had she made those men shatter like glass?

She shuddered a little. Greg hadn't just been right about her. He'd been psychic.

The staring contest lasted another five minutes before the dark man got up and came to stand by the tray. He picked up the bowl, dipped two fingers into it and stretched his arm out.

Althea didn't understand that he was trying to feed her until his fingers nearly touched her lips. She turned her head away and tried to retreat, grimacing as the chains of her shackles jerked on her sore legs.

He frowned and tried to feed her again.

"No," she said and glared up at him. "I don't want it. *Y*ou eat it."

The dark man went completely still, peering at her as if she'd told him to snort the oatmeal.

Maybe he didn't understand English. That seemed unlikely, although she'd heard of a couple of places where the locals spoke only in Scots Gaelic. But if she wanted to get out of here and find a police station, she had to get some kind of dialogue going.

"Maybe we should introduce ourselves. I'm Dr. Althea Jarden. Althea."

As she repeated her first name, she touched the base of her neck in emphasis. Gesturing at him, she gave him a quizzical look.

The dark man crouched down beside the bed. His expression seemed utterly absorbed, as if she were his favorite television show.

"Althea. My name is Althea. What's your name?" When he didn't respond she rubbed a hand over her brow. "Look, I'm a botanist, not a linguist. I have no idea how to say 'unchain me and let me go' in Gaelic. We have to find a way to talk." She studied him. "Are you deaf? Is that it?" She pointed to one of her ears and shook her head. "Can't hear me?"

He tilted his head to look at her ear before he went back to scrutinizing her face.

"Can you speak?"

She touched the front of her throat as she said that, and then scooted closer to reach out and press her fingertips to the same spot on his neck. The contact sent a rush of heat into her palm that raced over her wrist and up her arm.

His eyes narrowed, and he caught her hand as she drew it away. He held her gaze as he brought her fingers up to his mouth and held them against his lips.

Althea should have yanked her arm away, screamed, slapped him—something—but he wasn't acting like he wanted to violate her. She had the sense it was the exact opposite. Somehow he wanted to reassure her, maybe through the gentleness of his touch. Like saying, "Look, I don't bite."

"You're not a bad guy. I understand," she

said in a low, soothing tone. "Just say something. Anything."

He frowned.

Althea let the silence stretch for a few minutes before deciding that talking was not up for discussion—literally. "If you're on my side, if you're a good guy, then why chain me to the bed?" With her free hand she tugged on one shackle. "I'm not going to run away. I don't even know where we are. You can let me go."

The dark man's jaw tightened, and his brows drew together.

"Or I could stay." She shifted her fingertips from his mouth to his cheek. It felt a bit like petting an enormous wild animal, but maybe he needed some reassurance too. "You don't need the chains. I owe you my life. Did they take you too?"

He covered her hand with his and closed his eyes, his expression that of a man experiencing the best thing he'd ever felt.

Althea understood that. Touching his face made all her senses become suddenly acute. She could feel her heart capering like a skipping kid, and the rush in her blood bringing all her nerves to life. It felt scary, and sexy, a combination she'd never before felt. She couldn't resist shifting a little closer to him. Wherever she was, whatever he was doing, this man still attracted her like a fully-powered electromagnet.

From the way he was looking at her mouth, he felt the same pull.

"Hey," she said. "I know you saved me." On impulse she hugged him. "Thank you."

That turned him to stone, at least for three heartbeats. Then he drew back enough to slide his cheek against hers, and their mouths touched. Althea heard herself making a low, husky sound, and felt her hands tangling in his hair. Then they were kissing.

He didn't touch her, but his mouth went to town on hers. Heat suffused the air between them, and bursts of sensation rocked her body. She'd never been kissed with such hunger, or tasted such hot desire. He went at her like he'd been waiting his whole life for her, and had spent years dreaming of just this kiss. She felt herself go wet and pressed against him, unable to rationalize her reckless actions, but needing his touch on her swelling, aching breasts.

The dark man ended the kiss by standing and backing away from her toward the door. Now he looked ashamed, which made no sense at all.

"No, wait," Althea said, panting the words. "Don't go. I'm sorry. I shouldn't have— I don't know why I did that."

His mouth tightened, as if he felt the same way.

He understood what she was saying, Althea thought, but he couldn't or wouldn't respond. Maybe if she explained more of what had happened, he'd help her.

"I wasn't the only one out there. The people who took me still have four other women locked in a barn. One of them might be really sick." She didn't see a flicker of reaction on his face, so she gestured at him and then herself. "You and I, we have to save them."

Now he looked almost angry.

"We don't have to go back there," she said quickly. "Just let me call the police. I can tell them what happened, and you can draw a map to where we were."

The dark man shook his head and turned away.

"Wait." Althea tried to climb off the bed after him, only to fall on her face. "Please," she said pushing herself up from the floor, "if we don't do something, they're going to die out there. *Please*."

Chapter Nine

INSIDE THE FARMHOUSE in the woods the scents of apple and chamomile filled the kitchen as Hendry finished preparing a brew. After his long imprisonment in the Storr, he found performing the most ordinary tasks a pleasure. Waking in the farmer's bed beside his beloved allowed him to believe for a few moments that they had journeyed back another thousand years. They'd lived a beautiful, simple life among the Wood Dream tribe.

He would have that again with his lover, just as soon as they took their vengeance, and began their new tribe.

Murdina shared his vision, but she was easily distracted from it. The noises coming from the front room told him that his lover still paced about, kicking everything in her path. She'd been doing so ever since learning that one of the druidesses had escaped.

"How could this have happened? We put six on the barn to watch them, *six*. I ken that they're slower at night, but do they become totems again? If that little cloy-faced wench could slip away from so many, what hope have we?" Murdina stopped shouting for a moment, and the sound of pottery smashing combined with a wail of despair. "This shall ruin us, I ken it."

Hendry filled two cups, added a dollop of herbs and honey to one before he carried them out of the kitchen. "Here, firebrand mine. Your favorite blend. 'Twill ease your mood."

"Naught ever more, Hendry. That treacherous cow shall bring the Pritani to burn us out," Murdina raged. "Or the druids to bespell us again." She stopped and glared at the cup he held out to her, and then snatched it to take a deep swallow. "Do you wish to be trapped in stone for eternity? For 'tis what they'll do when they come. You and I and the *caraidean*, and they'll see to it that we cannae escape this time. They'll hurl us *into* the sun."

"You forget that they're helpless against us now, sweeting mine," he chided gently, and led her over to the fireplace, where he sat down with her huddled against his side. "We're made immortal, so their spells willnae work against us. They cannae enter this wood without our kenning it. As for the Pritani, aye, she may be clever enough to guide them to us. Let them come. We've an army of giants they cannae slay."

"But they shall ken we're returned and plot against us. They shall find another means to end us. Are you so great a fool that you cannae see it?" She drained her cup and got to her feet, swaying a little before she collapsed again and hunched her shoulders. "Oh, my love, I didnae mean to speak so harshly. 'Tis only that I cannae endure it again, even with you at my side." Turning to bury her face in his shoulder, she whimpered, "Dinnae let them take me. This time you must kill me."

"We didnae come back to die." Hendry stroked her silver-streaked curls. "The Gods freed us to continue our work, to make new the world. Our enemies shall have no place in it."

He held Murdina until she fell asleep, and then covered her with a woolen and watched her for a time. The herbs he'd added to her brew had calmed her, but soon they wouldn't be enough to stave off the madness. It was yet another horror for which Bhaltair Flen and his tribe would pay.

Outside the farm house Hendry found Aon standing in wait, his crackled face turned to the rising sun. "Forgive me for the delay. My lady has been most distressed."

Aon glanced through the window at the sleeping Murdina. "Part of her yet remains trapped in the Storr."

He hated himself for silently agreeing. "Did you find them?"

"The two the female destroyed, aye," the giant said as he gestured for the druid to accompany him. "They await new forms to be carved for them, and told the events of the night to me." As they walked through the trees Aon related what had happened, and then asked, "Why did she conceal her power?"

"Likely she wasnae aware of it," Hendry

BRENNUS   115

said. "In her time she possessed none. We ken that the groves change the druids they send through time. They acquire new talents and abilities. 'Twas why the conclave made it forbidden."

"There came another, the fallen told me," the giant said. "He moved like a bird, and wore the same on his flesh. The ink glowed blue."

Hendry suppressed a sour chuckle. "We saw the Skaraven die in your last battle, my friend, and watched them buried by Flen's lot. The warrior who aided the female couldnae be one of them. After so many ages, they're dust."

"The warrior took her with him into the lochan. He became as the water before he submerged." Aon halted in a patch of bright sunlight. "From it they vanished. Explain how they could."

Hendry glanced through the trees at the lochan. After their tribe had been murdered, he and Murdina had tried to convince the conclave to deliver justice for the Wood Dream. Too busy eluding the Romans and making bargains with the Pritani, they had refused.

"Before the invaders came to slaughter our tribe, Bhaltair Flen wished to give his mortal allies an advantage over the enemy," he told Aon. "Only a few druid like him could bestow such gifts. 'Tis likely this warrior's powers came from him. Once you take the warrior and the female, I shall question him."

"We cannae track the warrior," the giant said, his body ward shimmering with the sunlight he had absorbed. "No' through the lochan."

Hendry felt shaken by the reminder. How could he have been so foolish as to forget the *caraidean's* reaction to water? "Flen shall send more warriors soon. We must take Gwyn Embry and compel him to tells us where his old friend and the Dawn Fire now hide."

Aon shifted his gaze in the direction of the druid settlement on the other side of the mountain. "Good. Coig wants a new toy."

Chapter Ten

❦

THE DARK MAN didn't return to the chamber, and after an hour Althea started to worry. Hunger made her sample a little of the meal he'd left, to see if it made her sick or drugged. When it didn't she ate half the cold oatmeal and sipped a little of the water. If nothing else, being imprisoned had taught her to conserve food rations.

Why hadn't he come back yet?

"According to popular opinion, I *am* made of ice," Althea muttered under her breath as she tugged on the chains again. "Maybe kissing me made him so cold he needed a couple dozen hot toddies to warm up."

Her tingling lips throbbed a little, as if to disagree. The kiss, they assured her, had been the most heated, carnal experience of her short life. If it hadn't been his, *he* was a glacier. Any wild theory sounded better than the one she feared most.

What if he never comes back?

Althea released the chains and sat back, furious with herself for everything. Sure, she'd screwed up with men before now, but they were nothing compared to her colossal mistake in saving the dark man, and then kissing him. What kind of prisoner did that, anyway? Was she insane? Had she lost her mind and just didn't realize it?

No, she'd been born to crazy parents. She wasn't crazy. More likely she was hallucinating again.

"Hey." Grabbing one chain, Althea shook it so that it clanged against her shackles. If this was a hallucination, maybe she could freeze it like the guards. "Let me out of—" Her mouth snapped shut as the chain in her hand turned white and shattered. "Here."

She had enough sense not to touch the

frost-covered metal, which a few moments later entirely crumbled. The ankle shackle that had been attached to it now had a jagged gap from top to bottom. Watching the door and listening intently for a moment, Althea reached for the other chain, and held it tightly.

Nothing happened.

"Sorry, Greg," she muttered. "No career in the psychic trade for you."

She couldn't control a shiver as she pried off the broken shackle. It felt as if the room temperature had dropped thirty degrees, although the fire in the hearth still blazed. Something had flash-frozen the chain, and since she was the only one in the room it couldn't be her new captor. When she'd rapped the first chain against her shackles, she'd been thinking of the guards she'd frozen.

Telepathic freezing power? She felt disgusted with herself for even going there. "Come on, Althea. Think. You're a scientist, not a comic book fan. There has to be a rational explanation."

As rational as being dragged through the earth by a giant man made of wood, hurled into an abyss of spinning trees, and landing in a place that might just be fourteenth century Scotland? Rational explanations didn't work here.

Then try the irrational.

Althea tightened her grip on the chain as she made the same wish she had the first time. Frost bloomed on the metal links, turning them white as they cracked. This time she held on, and the chain dissolved and fell like snow from her fist. A sharp crack made her flinch, as the second shackle broke in two places.

Stunned now, she stared at the little pile of icy fragments. "I need to read more comic books."

After she removed the pieces of the shackle she rubbed her chilled fingers together. The back of her hand and her forearm also felt oddly cool. Every inch of her skin proved the same, as if she were suffering from a light case of exposure. Or maybe something had leeched the warmth from her flesh.

At college she'd hated the inorganic chem- istry, but now Althea thought back to what she'd learned during the metallurgy lab. If she had the power to alter the kinetic energy of the chains' atoms, enough to embrittle and shatter the iron, then her own tissue might have reacted.

"So, if I keep using it," she muttered, the thought sobering her. "I'll freeze too."

Althea climbed off the bed, gingerly walked around on the chamber's cold stone floor, and searched the room. She found a bundle of shabby, hand-sewn wool and linen clothing, all too large for her, next to three pairs of huge boots. After pulling on the smallest pair of pants, she tugged on the laces until she could tie them snug around her waist. Easing her battered legs into the clean-est-looking boots hurt, but the extra length of the trousers worked like stuffing. Taking a few wobbly steps, she pulled the blue silk coverlet from the bed and folded it into a long, wide rectangle. It slithered off her shoulders until she knotted the top two corners together under her chin.

Althea grimaced as she gazed down at the baggy outfit. She looked ridiculous, but hopefully it would keep her warm once she got outside.

The chamber's door had only a simple inside latch keeping it shut. When she released it the hinges groaned and the warped panel swung inward. Before she stepped through Althea looked out, checking both sides of the tunnel. Torches bracketed to the walls shed enough dim light to show her the emptiness of the passage.

Remembering the dark man turning right as he had carried her in, Althea went left. The hide boots soon worked their way down to wad around her ankles. Then she nearly slipped on a puddle of half-frozen water. Dressed like this, she was never going to make it through the woods. She had to have help. Frigid air poured around her as she passed a half-dozen chambers with sagging doors. Glancing up, she saw the torn canopy of dusty spiderwebs lacing the tunnel's rough-hewn ceiling. Everything she saw suggested the place to be ancient, huge, and deserted. An ideal location in which to hold someone prisoner, but it didn't look like a prison.

It felt mysterious, like some enormous secret.

Althea stopped at the next door she encountered, which fell inward the moment she touched it. The tremendous crash preceded a cloud of dust that she back-stepped to avoid. Guessing the noise would bring the dark man if he heard it, she didn't run. Instead she took down a torch and carried it inside.

Pulling the silk up to cover her nose and mouth, Althea turned around to inspect the room. Piles of decayed wood that had served as a bed, a small table and a chair lay heaped where they had collapsed. A large trunk had done the same, spilling out blackened rags. A collection of long rusty bars hung vertically on stone hooks on either side of the bed. It took a closer look for her to realize what they'd once been.

"Swords," Althea whispered and reached out to touch the pitted, ruined metal, which flaked beneath her fingertips. "Who lives like this?"

"The Skaraven, my lady," a deep voice answered.

He came up directly behind her, so close she could feel his body heat through her makeshift cloak. She turned to face him. This close the dark man towered over her, so big he blocked out the rest of the room. He'd changed into heavier clothing and boots, over which he wore a thick hooded cloak. Across his chest a thick leather strap ran from his shoulder to waist, and the unadorned hilt of a sword or knife glinted from behind his left shoulder. In his left hand he held her carryall.

"So you *can* talk." She wanted to slap him now, but that wouldn't help the situation. "Why did you pretend you couldn't?"

His dark brows drew together. "I wasnae pretending. I was…observing."

Lie, Althea thought. "Who are you? Why did you do this? You scared the wits out of me."

"I think no'." He pointed down at the boots she'd stolen. "You shatter chains and shackles. 'Tis no' the work of the witless."

His melodic Scottish accent sounded different from the mad druids', but he spoke in the same vernacular. Was he working with the lunatics after all?

"I want to call the police," she told him flatly. "Now."

"Naught you call can be heard from here." He plucked the torch from her hand before she could blink and sketched an odd sort of bow. "I'm Brennus, Chieftain of the Skaraven Clan." He offered her the carryall. "Come now, my lady, and I shall return you to your tribe."

She thought quickly as she took her bag. She could tell him that she didn't have a tribe, or she could get out of this place. "All right."

Brennus led her out of the room and down the passage to a newly-made wooden door, where he paused to remove his cloak. "You'll want this. 'Twill soon snow." He wrapped it around her and pulled the hood up over her hair.

The heavy wool still retained his body heat, which felt heavenly against her chilled skin. "How will you keep warm?"

One corner of his stern mouth curled. "Cold doesnae plague me, my lady." He opened the door, which revealed a narrow set of snow-covered stone steps lit from above. As a swirl of icy wind blew around them, he swept Althea off her feet and carried her up the stairs.

Cold certainly plagued her as Brennus emerged from the passage into a wintry forest of huge trees and rugged slopes. Althea spotted a river in the distance, but no lake or anything she recognized. She didn't see roads, cars, or any form of transportation waiting for them. The only sign that anyone had moved through the area were a few rough trails winding through the woods.

"Are we going on foot?" she asked as he set her down, and when he shook his head she sighed. "That's a relief. How close are we to where they were holding us? Will we pass a town or village where I can report this to the police?"

"I dinnae ken what 'tis police," Brennus said and scanned the horizon. "The druidesses arenae my clan's concern. You must speak to your tribe of it, my lady. Your elders may use their spells to free the others taken with you."

Althea felt an unnatural calm settle over her. What he said and the sincerity with which he said it finally convinced her. All the logic and science and rationality in the world would never explain Brennus, this place, or what had happened to her. "This is the fourteenth century."

"Aye." He studied her face. "'Tis no' your time."

"I won't be born for another seven centuries," she said and studied his calm face for a reaction. When none came the reserved tone of his voice finally sank in. "You're never going to help me, are you?"

"I cannae, my lady. My clan has suffered enough at the hands of the druids. I must protect my men." He nodded toward the river. "We should go now."

He was going to hand her over to more druids, just like that. After what the lunatics had done to her and the other women, no way in hell was Althea going anywhere with him.

"Right." She managed a willing smile. "Lead the way."

It fooled Brennus. Once he got far enough ahead of her, she turned and fled down one of the winding trails. Pain streaked through both of her legs, but she ignored it as she zig-zagged through the trees. The damn boots kept tripping her, so she reached down to jerk them up and glanced over her shoulder at the empty trail.

"I can do this," she muttered as she ripped the bandages from her hands and tied them around the boot tops.

Running in the heavy wool cloak made sweat streak down her back, stinging the wounds crisscrossing her spine. A few minutes later she felt a warmer dampness under the baggy trousers and guessed the running had reopened some of the gashes. She stopped to catch her breath and saw some small, dark patches soaking through the trousers. Brennus hadn't followed her, so she could risk walking for a little while.

The stabbing pain in her chest wasn't just due to the air temperature. It hurt to run away from him, and for the life of her Althea couldn't understand why.

The terrain grew steep as snowflakes began drifting down. She kept an eye out for any signs of civilization, but the forest and mountains seemed to go on forever. The dropping temperature made the air turn icy in her lungs. She turned around to check the trail again and saw that at least the snow was starting to cover her tracks. Soon he wouldn't be able to pick up her trail.

She'd be all alone out here. Alone and hurt.

"There'll be a village," she promised herself as she pushed on, and edged around a large leaf-filled depression in the ground. "A friendly farmer. Another clan that don't have issues with dru—"

Her feet stuttered to a stop as she saw Brennus waiting on the other side of the tree.

He looked just as happy to see her. "The river is the other way, my lady."

"I'm not your lady," she corrected. "I'm not your anything. Go back to your clan and do whatever is more important than the lives of four women. I'll find a village of nice people who care."

"On foot, 'tis a three-day walk to the nearest croft." He lifted his arm and pointed past her. "That way."

"Thanks for the directions." Althea turned around and grimly started back the way she came.

"You'll no' last another hour," Brennus told her as he kept pace with her wobbly steps.

"If the cold doesnae stop you, your bleeding shall."

She knew he was right. Her knees felt as unsteady as her head. She probably wouldn't make it another hundred yards. Admitting that, however, wasn't going to happen. "I don't care. I have to try."

Brennus caught her arm as she stumbled. "I cannae permit this, my lady."

"Then it's a good thing…you're not in charge of me."

She leaned against him, pressing her brow to his shoulder. Why were the trees spinning around her? It made her feel sick, and she didn't have time to throw up. She had to keep going. Yet when his arms enclosed her, her knees ignored her wishes and buckled.

"No," she breathed and pushed him away, staggering backward and shaking her head to clear it. "I'm not abandoning them to die. I'll never… stop trying. Now…get away…from…"

The world up-ended. Snow filled her eyes, mingling with the tears blinding her. Brennus held her against his chest as he carried her through the forest. By the time they arrived back at the entrance to the tunnels innumer-able snowflakes whitened his black hair.

Althea watched as they passed through a shaft of thin light, which made both of them glitter. For a moment the dark man looked so enchanting she wondered if it were all just a dream.

I should try to wake up, she thought, feeling completely muddled. *If I do, will I be back in the barn with the others?*

Only snatches of what happened next flashed through Althea's muddled confusion. Darkness pressed in on her as Brennus walked down the stone steps, which now seemed to descend for miles. She saw the flare of a torch and felt soft fur press on her aching back. Another, larger man with silvered dark hair spoke to the chieftain in a voice so deep her bones felt it. She smelled herbs and tasted something bitter that knocked her out almost instantly.

Waking up with a jerk, Althea rolled over onto her back. Someone had covered her with a blanket, but this time she wasn't in the chief-tain's chamber. She lay at the bottom of a deep, wide earthen pit with a mound of fleeces between her and the dirt floor. The trousers she'd stolen were gone, but fresh poultices and bandages had been applied to her wounds. The worn linen shirt she had on was different, and so long that it fell to her knees, but under it she was naked.

High above her a lighted circle hovered, shedding scant light on the room she now occupied. Perfectly round and entirely empty, it made her think of the bottom of a dried-up well. A rope ladder hung halfway down from the upper opening, too high for her to reach.

"Hello?" Her arms trembled as she pushed herself up. It took two tries to get on her feet. "Brennus?"

Calling for help produced no results, and she gave up to hobble around the pit. Just beneath the dangling rope ladder lay the bottom half. From the look of the ends it had been deliberately cut. Two buckets stood by a bundle of rags: one empty and the other filled with water. She didn't find any other way out, which made her peer up at the opening. On one side two hinges stuck out from the edge of a wooden trap door.

She'd been stuck in an oubliette.

Althea had once toured a chateau in France where one of the inescapable prison pits had been discovered. Death by confinement had been one of the worst medieval tortures. A prisoner dropped in an oubliette was "forgotten" by their captor and left to die of thirst and starvation.

"No." The word burst out of her, hard and absolute.

If Brennus had wanted her dead, he wouldn't have done this. He'd have bashed her head in, or just let her freeze to death outside. A killer wouldn't carry her back, redress her legs, and then stick her in a place she couldn't climb out. This was all way too much trouble.

"Oh, I get it," Althea muttered as she picked up the ladder's bottom half. "He didn't want me to escape again while he was off being chieftain and protecting his men. Jerk." She threw the hacked-off rope away from her, and heard a splash as it landed in the filled bucket. "And now my only water supply's polluted."

She plucked the rope out of the bucket, and then stared at the dripping hemp. Shaking it out straight, she saw that it was a good six feet long.

"*Stupid* jerk." She laughed. "You left me a get-out-of-jail-free card."

Althea couldn't risk destroying her only out, so she picked up some fleece and thought of freezing it, just enough to make it stiff. The soft curls slowly frosted over, growing stiff, but when she touched them they didn't break. A chill also raced over her flesh, but not as cold as when she had frozen the first chain.

"One more time."

She went over to the water bucket and dipped her fingertips into it. As soon as she thought of a thin layer of ice, crystals spread out from her hand. They continued thickening when she pulled her fingers out until a quarter-inch of clear ice sealed over the water.

Her breath came out in an opaque cloud as she stared down at the bucket. "What do you know? I can control this thing."

The rope ladder end creaked as she froze the fibers stiff, and leaned it against the side of the pit. Looking up, she measured the distance from the top of the frozen rope ladder to the end of the one hanging from the opening.

She'd have to stretch a bit, but she could reach it. Hanging the blanket around her neck, she started climbing up her iced ladder.

The frozen hemp cracked under Althea's body weight, and for a moment she thought it might collapse. She grabbed the sides and froze it a little more, imagining it with a thick coating of ice. The cold backlash became more intense, making the air in the pit go frigid. She also lost the feeling in her fingers, nose and ears, but she clambered to the top. Balancing on her toes, she stretched her numb hand toward the rope hanging above her. Just as she caught hold of it the iced ladder slipped out from under her, and she lunged, seizing the rope with her other hand.

"Damn it." The hemp dug into Althea's palms and fingers as she dangled. If she fell she'd probably break a limb, so letting go wasn't an option. "Okay, don't panic. Don't think. Just move."

The chilly numbness helped as she hauled herself up and the rough rope abraded her skin. By the time she climbed high enough to get a foothold her hands had been rubbed raw and bloody.

"I really hate the fourteenth century." She took a minute to wind two corners of the blanket around them before she reached for the next rung.

At the top she peeked over the edge of the oubliette's opening. On either side stretched another stone passage lit by a few torches, but she saw no sign of anyone else.

Slinging the blanket out first, Althea grabbed the two hooks holding the ladder's end and hoisted herself out of the oubliette. Landing with a painful flop on her belly, she crawled another foot and rolled over to stare at the dark red rocks above her.

"When we get back, I can moonlight as an escape artist."

She pulled her hands from the blanket to survey the damage. Hemp fibers protruded from some nasty rope burns, and red shiny blisters had popped up on her knuckles and joints. For a minute she didn't understand, and then the pins and needles set in.

She'd given herself frostbite.

Screaming would just get her caught and tossed back into the pit, so she clenched her teeth and forced herself to think. The other women were depending on her. She couldn't try to walk out again, not in the condition she was in. That left finding Brennus, or one of his clan, and forcing them to take her to someone who would help her.

To do that, she needed a weapon.

Chapter Eleven

WORKING MOST OF the day alongside his men gave Brennus the opportunity to calm their agitation. As they cut each other's hair with Kanyth's shears, he answered their questions about Althea honestly, but also carefully. Volunteering such details as the old Roman word she'd called herself—doctor— would only alarm the clan. He also didn't reveal her powerful ability or that she had been taken from a distant future.

Leaving her alone in the *eagalsloc* had taken all of his resolve, but it was the only place in the stronghold from which she couldn't escape. Ruadri had helped lower them both into the pit and then hauled Brennus back out once the chieftain had settled her. He'd grown angry only when he saw he'd cut the rope ladder.

"Are you crazed?" the shaman had demanded. "None can climb out of a fear pit. She's wounded and helpless."

"Hurt, aye, but not helpless," Brennus said and shook his head. "Time in the *eagalsloc* 'twill do her no harm. I'll fashion another ladder and bring food to her after sunset."

Ruadri's mouth tightened as he stared down at Althea. "She belongs with her tribe, no' here."

"She claims no tribe and denies she's druid kind. She swore to me she wouldnae stop trying to escape." When Ruadri would have argued Brennus lifted his hand. "Her power destroyed the bodies of two *famhairean* with a touch. She can do the same to our brothers."

"So into the fear pit, where she cannae touch anyone," Ruadri gave him a narrow look. "What of you? She put hands on you, and naught happened."

If only the shaman knew, Brennus thought. "'Tis done. Until I decide what to do with her, she stays in the *eagalsloc*."

Ruadri had stalked off after that, and for the rest of the day avoided Brennus. Being at odds with the shaman didn't sit well with him, nor did the tangle of his thoughts. By her own admission Althea Jarden didn't belong in this time. She should be returned to her own by the druids. But could they be trusted to do so? As powerful as she was, Brennus knew Althea couldn't destroy all the *famhairean* at once. Any attempt by her to return to the mountain and confront her captors would end with her dead.

The chieftain refused to sacrifice his clan again, but he could not stomach the thought of Althea dying either. By day's end he knew he would have to seek direction from the one source he trusted without question. He headed to the clan's *caibeal*. The small chapel lay in Dun Mor's lowest level at the far end of the passage leading to the *eagalsloc*. The chapel's door, hand-carved by the clan's quarriers from a single slab of granite, swung inward without resistance. It had sealed the inner chamber so well that the only sign that twelve centuries had passed was the tiny piles of dust that had once been watchlights.

Brennus placed his torch in a stone bracket

by the entry and walked through the outer cross slabs to the center, where the largest stood. Hewn from a giant morion, the blackest of crystals, it depicted a raven at rest, its head turned to watch its back.

Seeing once more the image of his battle spirit made Brennus cover his right shoulder with his hand. Beneath his tunic his skinwork began to move, stabbing into his flesh like the gouging of a sharp beak. He knelt before the stone and spread his hands.

"I dinnae ken why I live, only how I must," he said, pulling his tunic over his head to bare his chest. "'Tis been many lifetimes since last I came to you, but I ask now for your guidance. I owe a life-debt to Althea Jarden. I owe my loyalty to my clan. I dinnae ken which path to take."

The pain in his shoulder went deeper, but Brennus ignored it and kept his gaze on the stone raven. He knew he did not possess Ruadri's unwavering faith in the gods, but his battle spirit had been a part of his flesh and heart since boyhood. It had never once abandoned him, although now it seemed to be boring a hole through his body, while the raven stone remained cold and dark.

"I didnae ask for death, nor this awakening." He rose as the ink writhed on his shoulder like a living thing. "But your warrior shall I ever be."

The torch suddenly extinguished, and the skinwork on his chest lit up with a dark blue glow. All around him the air moved, thick with unseen spirits. Yet when the torch flared back to life Brennus found himself alone, and unanswered.

"Naught, then." All of the anger he'd held back since returning from the grave broke free. "Fack you for it."

His curse rang out in the *caibeal*, but before he could stalk out shadows rose from the raven stone. Taking on the shape of his battle spirit, they flew in a tight circle just above his head. They swooped to attack him, their sharp beaks hammering into his scalp, shoulders and arms. Brennus batted them away from his eyes, but he refused to cower. If the raven spirit wished to devour him alive, it had better be very hungry.

A sharp cry scattered the spirits, and

Brennus echoed it as Althea came running toward him.

"Stop it." She rushed toward Brennus, waving her arms in the air to ward off the ravens. The moment she touched one it hurtled up to join what rapidly grew into a seething cloud of darkness. "What are these things?" She lifted her gaze and went still. "Oh, no."

Brennus eyed the huge raven shape, which began descending toward them. "My thanks, lass, but you must go. Quickly now."

Instead of obeying, Althea put herself between him and the battle spirit.

"Leave him alone," she told the enormous raven as it hovered before her. "That goes for me too. I don't know what you are, but that's like everything here, so fine. Go beat the crap out of someone else. I suggest you start with those crack-faced mutant things that dragged me back to this godforsaken time."

The huge raven surged forward and, though she flinched, it perched on her shoulder. She didn't move. "Or you could just not beat anyone. How's that sound?"

The manifestation of his battle spirit

spread its wings wide, and then curled them around Althea, who gasped. A moment later the raven dissolved into smoke, and Brennus caught her before she hit the floor.

"I'm okay." She extracted herself from his arms. "Don't tell me what that was, please. Just don't." She frowned and lifted her hands to inspect them. "Wait a minute. This is weird."

Brennus saw the dried blood on her hands but no wounds. "You're hurt."

"I was hurt. Climbing out of your oubliette gave me a bad case of rope burn." Althea rubbed her palms together. "They're gone." She reached down to pull away the bandage on her thigh. "My legs are healed, and I think my back is too." She moved her shoulders as if uncomfortable. "This shirt is a bit heavy, is all."

Brennus reached out to touch the black crystal. Battle spirits held sway over the flesh of those Pritani they chose, but he'd never heard of one healing druid kind. He'd asked for guidance, and it had been clearly given. The raven had chosen to help Althea. So, too, would he.

"My thanks," Brennus said to the stone before turning to her. "Forgive me, my lady. I shouldnae have denied you. I'll take you to the great hall, where you may speak to my clan about the others, where you were kept, and anything you ken about your captors and their camp. Then we shall plan how to free those still held."

"Finally," she exhaled. "Thank you." She turned to go, but stopped and glanced back at him. "You cut your hair."

Chapter Twelve

✦❧✦

AFTER SURVIVING TIME travel, killer roots, and the bird attack in the room of big carved rocks, Althea felt meeting the rest of the Skaraven would be a breeze. That assurance evaporated the moment she and Brennus walked into a cavernous area occupied by immense, tattooed men.

She forgot to blink as she took in the small army of warriors. Built on a mammoth scale, their bodies had been so well-developed she could see every bulging muscle under their poorly-fitted garments. Every Skaraven stood well over six feet, with oversized hands, long-yoked shoulders, and clearly powerful limbs.

Most wore their newly shorn hair close-cropped, like Brennus. He had told her it was to keep their vision clear in battle and not give an enemy something to grab.

The men, who had been busy working on various tasks and projects, all stopped and stared at her. The intensity in their eyes reminded her both of starving wolves and dazzled teenagers.

"This is Lady Althea Jarden," Brennus said, his voice booming in the utter silence. "The *famhairean* took her and four other females from the future. She escaped them and later stopped two from ending me. In return for the life-debt, she asks that the clan help free those still held." He eyed someone at the back of the assembled men. "I asked for guidance, and my raven spirit healed her wounds."

The men didn't make a sound, but Althea thought from the way they all looked at each other that the raven healing was a big deal.

"'Tis my intent to rescue the four lasses still held by the *famhairean*, and to find the means to defeat them forever." Brennus looked around the hall. "What says the clan? Do you join me?"

"Bràithrean an fhithich," the men roared, thrusting their right fists into the air.

The chieftain met her gaze. "The brethren of the Skaraven agree, my lady."

Although their shouts startled Althea, their lack of hesitation made her smile. They might look like an army of medieval mercenaries, but their willingness to fight to free the others made it clear that they had good hearts. She also found it interesting that the clan had been given a choice by Brennus, not what she would have expected in this era.

"My thanks," she said to the clan, remembering her manners and the way Brennus had expressed his gratitude to her. "If there's anything I can do, please tell me."

Some of the men shared odd looks, while others chuckled.

"She speaks of the quest," Brennus said, making a cutting gesture, which silenced the clan as all eyes returned to him. "Name yourselves to the lady."

What followed had to be the strangest

mass introduction Althea had ever experi-
enced. Nearly all of the clansmen assembled
into ten lines, and each one marched up to
take a knee in unison before her and the chieftain. Each one then stood and said two words
before retreating to reform their line.

"Bridei, Woodsman."

"Ailpin, Hunter."

"Manath, Flamekeep."

At first Althea thought they were giving
her their full names. After several repetitions,
the noticeable pauses, and some very odd
surnames, it finally dawned on her. Bridei's
last name wasn't Woodsman, he *was* a
woodsman.

The last four men to introduce themselves
came from behind the ranks and took positions in front of them like leaders. They
bowed but didn't kneel or speak.

"My advisors and clanmasters," Brennus
murmured to her before he nodded to them,
and they gave their name and position.

She recognized Ruadri, the shaman and
the largest man in the hall. Weapons Master
Kanyth looked so much like Brennus she

guessed they were related. Taran spoke so
softly that she barely heard him, and Cadeyrn
looked at her as if she were a bug. Her back
started to tingle oddly, making it hard to stand
still.

"I'm very glad to meet all of you," she told
the men.

Instead of dismissing them, Brennus told
the men to gather, and they moved out of
their ranks to crouch in a large, perfect circle
around Althea. Kanyth brought a wooden
stool for her to sit on before he dropped down
at her right side along with Ruadri. Taran and
Cadeyrn did the same at Brennus's left.

"Tell the men how you came to be here,
my lady," the chieftain said.

Althea had never been adept at group
speaking, and being surrounded by so many
big men was intimidating. But lives depended
on this, so she did her best to describe how
she'd been taken and the events that had
followed. She felt a little ridiculous as she
detailed the strange freezing power she had
acquired, but none of the Skaraven laughed at
her. She did notice the hatred that flared in

almost every face when she spoke of the strange men working with the druid couple.

"I'm convinced that the guards aren't human," Althea finally said. "They may look like men on the surface, but they're something else." She turned to the chieftain, shimmying her shoulders to try to stop the now seriously annoying tingling. "You called them the *famhairean*. What does that mean?"

"Giants," Brennus said. "A druid tribe fashioned them from fallen sacred oaks into statues of immense warriors. They placed them around their village and their ritual meadow to frighten away invaders. 'Twas thought over time the tribe's magics changed them from dead wood to living creatures. They came fully to life after Romans massacred the Wood Dream. They've been killing mortal and druid kind ever since."

"So, they were trees first," Althea said. She pushed aside her disbelief and thought for a moment. "That explains why they're so heavy and awkward, and their faces are cracked, like oak bark. Are they made entirely of wood?"

The chieftain gestured to Ruadri, who said, "The bodies they inhabit, aye, my lady.

The life within them, no. Like the sacred grove that brought you to this time, they are eternal. Immortal."

Althea flashed back to her memory of falling through the tunnel of writhing branches. Then a new realization dawned on her and she shivered.

"Then the two giants that attacked your chieftain aren't dead," she said. She looked up at the rest of the clan, and suddenly realized the enormity of what she was asking of the Skaraven. "Can anything destroy them?"

"We dinnae ken, my lady," Ruadri said. "The druids trapped their spirits in a wood henge to remain imprisoned for all time. Yet somehow they escaped."

"Something in the future must have smashed the henge," Kanyth put in.

"The geomagnetic disturbance unleashed by the solar storm could have been the culprit," she said and saw the Weapons Master's expression and grimaced. "Sorry. I'm a scientist in my time, but that won't make sense to anyone for another five hundred years. What I mean is, a change in the sun's brightness probably caused the henge to fail."

Surreptitiously she reached behind her to rub the prickling spot on her back, but to her frustration she couldn't reach it.

"The *famhairean* draw power from the daylight," Ruadri told her. "'Tis their food. Darkness makes them weak."

"Lily said they were slower at night. She's one of the other women." She gave up scratching her back and sighed. "The *famhair* who took her almost strangled her."

"The giants always kill mortals who cross their path," Cadeyrn said suddenly. "Why did they take five of you? Why let you live after you crossed over into this time?"

Here was the clan's skeptic, Althea thought. "They said they needed druid kind to open the time portal. I also think that they still needed us for something more, but what I can't say. None of us are druids, ah, druidesses, but it's possible that we're their descendants." She glanced at Brennus. "I'm really not sure why they needed five of us."

"Reserves, mayhap," Kanyth said. "If one dies, another takes her place."

Before Althea could ask him to elaborate Brennus said, "'Tis growing late. We shall begin preparations on the morrow." As the men rose he gestured to Ruadri. "The lady requires your attendance."

Aside from the sensitive spots on her back Althea felt fine, but she was curious about the clan's healer, so she accompanied him and Brennus to another chamber adjoining the great hall.

As Ruadri lit some greasy plant stalks that served as candles, Althea discreetly inspected the room. Like the great hall it had been sparsely furnished, but rows of chiseled symbols and pictographs covered the stone walls. Ancient-looking stone vessels and pots had been carefully collected in one corner of the floor. Rendered fat, probably for making salves, quivered white on a curved plank of newly-cut wood. Bundles of plants and flowers hung to dry from a rack made of tree branches tied together with vines. She recognized heather, self-heal and yarrow, and smelled the distinct scent of cyclamen coming from a cluster of unfamiliar, broad green leaves.

"What is this, Shaman?" she asked Ruadri, and pointed to the bunch.

"One-bloom mint," the shaman told her, and showed her a large, white flower he had dried. "'Tis good for clouded eyes." He gestured toward the long, wide table covered with sacking. "Will you sit, my lady?"

Althea perched on the edge. "The herbal poultice you used on my legs worked almost as well as the raven spirit."

"Aye, 'tis better than staunch weed. If I may look?" When she nodded Ruadri eased up the end of the trousers Brennus had given her.

The only sign that she had been wounded were some flecks of dried blood that still clung to her skin. When the shaman brushed them away her flesh looked completely unmarked.

"As I reckoned," the shaman told her after checking the other leg. "Spirit healings dinnae close the wounds as much as scour them away."

"So no scars," she said and leaned down, and then jumped as Ruadri jerked away from her. "It's all right. I just wanted to take a better look myself. Is there some kind of clan taboo about touching a shaman?"

"None, my lady." He turned away from

her and fussed with some of his herbs while he gave Brennus a direct look. "Chieftain, if you would raise the back of her tunic."

"I can do that," Althea said and pulled up the chunky hem and folded it over her shoulders before she presented her back to the men. "How does it look? The same as my legs?" When neither man said anything she glanced over her shoulder. "It feels almost like I have a sunburn, but it doesn't hurt... Why are you two staring at me like that?"

"Your back wounds are healed, my lady," the shaman said slowly. He started to say more, stopped and shook his head. "Chieftain."

"I ken. 'Tis for me." Brennus nodded at the entry to the chamber, and Ruadri abruptly departed.

Althea dropped the tunic and turned around to face the chieftain. "What's wrong? Why did you send him away?" Her eyes widened as he pulled off his tunic. "Brennus, wait."

"Only to be sure," he said, and drew her to her feet. He took hold of her hand, and pressed it over the raven tattoo on his shoulder.

The tingling on Althea's back vanished, replaced by a sweet warmth that slowly seeped through her skin and wrapped around her torso. Heat flooded her breasts and her face, and she could feel her cheeks reddening from it. At the same time she felt something move under her palm.

"My lady," Brennus said and tightened his hand over hers.

"I feel it." She shifted closer to him, unable to bear even the small gap between their bodies. "It's like when we kissed…just so much stronger. Will you stop calling me 'my lady', please? I want to hear you say my name."

"I shouldnae." He cradled her cheek with his other hand. "But I will." He tilted her head back to look into her eyes. "Althea."

No one had ever said her name with such soft, deep pleasure.

"I'm actually named after a flowering plant," she murmured, rubbing her cheek against his palm. "*Althaea officinalis.* The common marshmallow." A chuckle slipped from her lips. "The ancient Egyptians boiled the plant's root pulp with honey to soothe sore throats. Two thousand years later, we roast the candy version over campfires." She paused and looked into his eyes. "Brennus."

Gentle heat warmed her cheek where his palm caressed it.

"'Twill pass," he said, though he didn't sound too certain.

"This is coming from you," she murmured, her eyelids drooping. "Some kind of magic again? God, it feels so good."

"'Tis no' my doing, my lady." He released her hand, and some of the heat ebbed away. "The raven did heal the wounds on your back, but there are scars. They form the shape of my battle spirit." He touched his ink. "The same as my skinwork does."

"So I have a scar version of your tattoo on my back?" When he nodded she felt weirdly elated. "Why would it completely heal my legs but not my back?"

Brennus put his tunic on before he replied. "The raven has chosen you, my lady. It marked you as its own."

Whatever he was feeling seemed to be

rolling off him in dark waves, and it wasn't the sleepy desire she felt. Was he angry? Offended? Had she somehow blown the chance to free the others? That last thought acted like a bucket of icy water on her head, clearing her mind of the somnolent longing.

"I don't understand," Althea said carefully. "Why would it do that? I'm not one of you. I don't even belong in this time." When he didn't respond she said, "If this is inappropriate, then maybe I should talk to one of the women in your clan."

"The Skaraven have none," the chieftain said. "Females were forbidden to us."

"What?" Her jaw dropped. "My God, why?"

"The tribes who sired us did so to use us as warrior-slaves. We were property, not free men." His voice grew bitter. "They kept us secluded, away from all others. They didnae wish us to breed, and they believed us too dangerous to be trusted with females, so we were forbidden to take wives or even be near females."

Suddenly she understood, and it appalled her. "That's why the men stared at me like that. Why Ruadri was so afraid to touch me. You and your clan have never known *any* women?"

"Before you came," Brennus said, almost sadly. "We had never spoken to one."

Chapter Thirteen

IN THE REMOTE ridges of the northern highlands, Bhaltair Flen stood in the small garden behind his cottage to watch the moon rise. Contemplating the night sky bejeweled by stars that twinkled their welcome to that lovely pearl of the Gods had always calmed him. His heaviest cloak warded off most of the night wind's bite, and the comforting brew he'd sipped earlier still warmed his belly and soothed the aches of age.

But nothing could dispel the chill of knowing that somewhere out in the darkness the *famhairean* hunted mortal kind.

Spurred on by their endless rage, and the two thousand years they had spent imprisoned, they had grown even more vicious. The innocents slain now numbered in the hundreds. Their watchers to the west had reported finding corpses so mercilessly tortured that to look upon them made the strongest stomach empty.

Awakening the Skaraven had been the only solution. No other clan knew the giants as they did, and none possessed the savage skills with which to fight them. From the time Bhaltair had agreed to help train the indentured lads, he'd sensed they would someday sorely need the warriors they became to protect mortal and druid kind. Now his faith in the Skaraven had become his punishment. Even the constant, miserable throbbing of his bad leg did not hurt as much as seeing their only hope turn their backs on him. The last, scathing reply from their chieftain still rang in Bhaltair's ears.

We're no' your slaves anymore. Clean up your own cac.

Feeling his leg tremble, Bhaltair leaned heavily on his cane as he limped over to his garden bench. Tomorrow he would have to go before the conclave and confess his failure.

Whatever unpleasantness and punishment came from it, he would accept without protest. Perhaps the elders would be kind enough to imprison *him* in a henge for all eternity.

"Master Flen," a low voice called. "Forgive my intrusion, but I bring news."

He looked up to see one of the conclave's acolytes hovering at his back gate. His youth reminded him too much of Ovate Lusk, now gone to the Gordon stronghold to protect his very important, half-druid son and the mortal family that nurtured the bairn.

Gods, how he missed Cailean. "Come and deliver it, lad."

The young druid entered and hurried over to him, bowing before he handed him a small, stained message scroll. "'Twas found on the body of a murdered elder."

Bhaltair unrolled it and read.

Brother Flen, you must move the Dawn Fire to the islands or they shall soon perish. Those who walk the path of vengeance seek you and yours now.

He stared at the precise handwriting, which he had seen in countless messages and letters from the west. On his back, a faded spell ward had been written by the same hand. "No. No' Gwyn Embry."

"'Twas he they found killed." The young druid sat down beside him. "He went missing from his settlement threeday past."

"Why was I no' told of this?" Bhaltair demanded.

"Word reached us only now, Master." He looked down at his hands. "The watchers say he must have been taken by the giants. Only they could make him suffer for so long before he disincarnated. They kept him two days—"

"No more." Bhaltair crumpled the message in his shaking fist. "Leave me." When the boy didn't move he shouted, "Begone with you."

The young druid murmured an apology before he hurried off. A moment later a light rain began to fall.

This wretched incarnation had become too much to bear, Bhaltair thought, leaning back and closing his eyes as the cold droplets pelted him. To think he'd prided himself on how much he'd accomplished since returning from the well of stars to begin this lifetime.

Sharing the wisdom gained from his many

incarnations with the young among his tribe, he'd assured that they would serve druid kind with devotion and vigor. Countless times he'd intervened to assure that their mortal and immortal allies remained closely bound. He'd trained Cailean, a promising ovate who had become a treasured companion as well as a fearless champion for good. From a distant future the Gods had brought to Bhaltair the last of his blood kin, whom he had grown to love as a daughter born to him. At great personal risk he'd fought monstrous, abiding evil again and again. For his efforts he'd risen to a position of respect among druid kind unmatched by any other elder of his stature.

But how could he abide knowing that his oldest, most beloved friend had left this world so cruelly? Tears mixed with rain and fell from his blurry eyes as he stared once more at the crumpled message. So easy it would be to blame the Skaraven for this, but the fault lay with him. How could he live with the knowledge that but for his pride he might have prevented Gwyn's horrific death?

Footsteps approached on the garden stone path, and Bhaltair pressed his sleeve over his wet face. "You neednae worry on me, lad. Send the watcher who brought the scroll to me on the morrow. I must have time to grieve for my old friend tonight."

"I'm no' a lad or a watcher, Master," a sweet voice said.

A very young druidess appeared in front of him. Short and plump, the lass had a child-like face framed by bedraggled, dripping brown hair. Her big dark eyes reminded him of a curious doe staring out of the woods.

She bobbed, her wet boots squishing as she said, "I brought the message found on my grandfather's body. I ken that he would wish you to have it."

Bhaltair knew from Gwyn's many letters that he had but one grandchild. "You're Oriana Embry?"

She ducked her head as the shower grew heavier. "That 'tis my name, Master."

"Gwyn wrote of you with much affection." His cane wobbled as he rose. "Come in out of the rain, dear one."

"Permit me, Master." Oriana took his other arm and helped him through the back door. Once inside she took his cloak and had him sit at his dining table.

"You're very young to be making such a journey, lass," Bhaltair said as he watched her hang their cloaks to dry by the hearth.

He knew that her parents had died of the sweating sickness just after her birth. They'd had no siblings, nor had she. Her grandfather and his tribe had raised her.

She went into the kitchen, fetched a goblet of water, and placed the drink in front of him. He took a sip and gestured for her to sit. "You ken that your headman will attend to your training and place you with a good family."

"Grandfather already arranged it. I'm to dwell with two sisters who take in the tribe's orphans." She started to bite the nail of her thumb, stopped herself, and tucked her hands in the ends of her sleeves. "Master, my grandfather asked me to come to you if he died. He directed me to speak for him."

Bhaltair frowned. "I dinnae ken your meaning."

"I must first open my heart as passage." She placed her hands flat on the table, bowing her head and murmuring under her breath.

He reached out to touch her hand, which she snatched away from him. "Oriana?"

The table rocked as her body shook uncontrollably, and then went still. When she raised her face her eyes had gone white, and her sweet, trusting expression had turned sharp and knowing.

"She's no' sick, you old curmudgeon," she said in a much deeper, hauntingly familiar voice. "You'll be, if you dinnae put on a dry robe."

I've gone mad, Bhaltair thought, pressing his fingers over his mouth.

"You've naught to say to your brother initiate?" the eerie voice coming from the girl's mouth demanded. "'Twas no silencing you when we were lads. I recall you swearing you'd never become the conclave's creature on the night we pledged ourselves before the elders. You'd more to do with your magics than caper to their tune, you vowed. And now look at you. You've but to whistle, and they dance for *you.*"

"Oh, Gods." He dropped his hand. "'Tis you, Gwyn."

"Aye, you great lassie's skirt." Her grandfather's raspy laugh ruffled the air. "I told Oriana that if I died badly to come to you, and thus summon me. Poorly isnae the word for what I suffered." Her lower lip trembled. "'Twas monstrous, what they did to me, Bhaltair. But I never spoke a word to them. You may be sure of that."

Fear iced over his shame. "Gwyn, never tell me that you've possessed your own blood kin."

"Fie, the spew you wretch," his dead friend scolded. "Oriana channels spirits from the well of stars. Dinnae gape at me. I wrote to you of her gift no' three months past. The lass may prove to be the most powerful speak-seers among druid kind."

"So you shall release her and return to the well when we've done speaking." As she nodded Bhaltair let out a long breath. "I'm to blame for your murder, old friend. 'Twas my duty to awaken the Skaraven and convince them to again protect us against the *famhairean*. I brought them back but failed to persuade them to join our cause. In truth, I reckon I drove them away."

"I dinnae fault you, pledge-brother."

Oriana's expression turned shrewd. "And as long as the Skaraven still walk your world you havenae failed. You must seek them out and convince them to take up this new quest. Only through them can my killing be avenged, and mortal and druid kind be made safe."

Bhaltair didn't relish the thought of bracing the Skaraven again. "You've more faith in me than is wise. I cannae—"

"You must." Hot color flooded into Oriana's face while Gwyn's voice went from a shout to a cold murmur. "Unless you find the Skaraven, we are doomed. All of mortal and druid kind shall be exterminated. Without bairns for our rebirth, we shall be trapped in the well of stars until the end of time."

Oriana suddenly slumped over and went limp, only to push herself up a moment later. Her soft doe eyes met his worried gaze.

"He's gone away," she whispered in her own, sweet voice as she pressed a trembling hand to her brow. "Oh, my poor grandfather. He's so frightened, Master."

Bhaltair offered her the water, which she refused. He fetched some *uisge beatha* from his cabinet. She drank a small measure of the whiskey, coughing a little as she stared at her hands.

"Did you ken what was said while you channeled Gwyn's spirit?" He felt relieved when she shook her head. "You havenae used your gift often, have you, lass?"

"No, Master Flen. 'Twas no one among the tribe to train me but Grandfather, and he wished me first to pledge myself as a novice and learn more control. Sometimes I couldnae help speaking for the dead." Her lips twisted. "Like him, they can be very determined."

"'Twas Gwyn who kept me on the path when we were initiates," Bhaltair told her. "I sometimes think he taught me more than even the wisest of our masters. You should be very proud to carry on his bloodline, my dear one."

"Aye. I loved him so." She choked on the words, and then summoned a tremulous smile. "I must return to my settlement, so I will leave you now. I shallnae forget your kindness, Master Flen."

"Stay the night here." He surprised himself by blurting out the offer, and grimaced. "'Tis late, and I have a spare bed." He gestured toward his small guest room.

"'Twould ease my thoughts to ken you safe under my roof until daylight."

"And mine." Oriana looked relieved. "'Tis always tiring to use my gift. My thanks, Master."

Once she had settled down to sleep Bhaltair changed into a dry robe and went into his spell chamber. At first he meant only to meditate on what Gwyn had urged him to do, but his thoughts kept straying back to the past they had shared. In his first lifetime Bhaltair had been an impatient boy, gripped by the untapped power inside him and anxious to wield it. When the short, pudgy Gwyn Embry had joined his initiate circle, Bhaltair had barely noticed, so focused had he been on the druids teaching them.

"You'll no' learn to cast spells until after you're pledged, no matter how long you tag-tail after the masters," Gwyn had told him one day as they gathered herbs for an ovate teaching them healing potions. "They dinnae trust the uninitiated with proper magics." He waggled his brows. "But I ken a trick or two."

Bhaltair remembered how he'd sniffed his contempt and turned away from him, only to find himself facing a monstrous black and white serpent with blazing red eyes and fangs dripping venom. The creature had to be twenty feet long, and loomed up over him as if it meant to devour him with a single bite.

Gwyn came to stand beside him. "'Tis really no' so grand." He tossed some myrtle at the snake, which hissed and shrank down to a tiny baby adder, which wriggled away into the grass. "My gran taught me that one to scare wolves away from our herds."

"We're no' permitted to use tribe magic," Bhaltair said, still staring after the snake. "You could be sent home for such."

"Aye, if you tell." Gwyn grinned. "Shall I teach you the spell, then?"

They had been inseparable after that day, Bhaltair remembered as he blew out the lamps and made his way to his bed chamber. He stopped outside the guest room to listen for a moment, and heard a soft sobbing. He rested his hand against the door, wishing he could do anything to comfort the lass.

Why had Gwyn tasked her to come to him? Their friendship had been long and filled with much affection, but Oriana was far too young and unskilled to be away from her tribe. Surely he could have left instructions with an acolyte, or even an ovate.

Bhaltair slept fitfully until the hour just before dawn, when he abandoned his bed and went to brew a morning blend with some yarrow for his aching head. He knew in their former lifetime the Skaraven had built a secret stronghold somewhere in the Red Hill Mountains, but no one had ever seen it or knew of its location. Since all of the clan's mortal allies had died long ago, he would have to journey south to the border of the old Skaraven territory. There he might arrange a meeting with the only druid ally left to him—if the man chose to answer his summons.

"Fair morning, Master Flen," Oriana said. She came into the kitchen, her hair in beribboned braids and her eyes still faintly swollen from weeping. "How good that smells."

"'Twill taste better than the whiskey, at least." He poured a mug for her, adding a bit of honey to sweeten the brew. "So tell me, will the sisters who take you in begin your training soon?"

"I dinnae reckon so. They tend the herds

for the tribe." She forced a smile. "I do like sheep, and I'm sure I shall learn much about caring for them."

To put the lass to work as a shepherdess when she had such power seemed ridiculous to him. "Oriana, does your tribe have another speak-seer among them?"

"No, Master," she admitted. "I think Grandfather meant to foster me to another tribe for my training. He spoke of an old friend from his first incarnation."

Here was the true reason the lass had been sent to him. "That would be me, my dear one." As her eyes widened he patted her hand. "Now it comes clear to me why we were brought together. Gwyn intended for me to teach you."

She paled. "Oh, Master, never say 'tis such. I'm no' worthy of your wisdom. I– I ken naught of magic."

"'Tis why I must teach you, Oriana." He had never taken an acolyte so young, nor a female, but given the potential of her power she sorely needed his guidance. She also deserved to play a part in seeking justice for Gwyn's murder. "I must journey today to the southern highlands to find the Skaraven Clan. 'Twill no' be an easy or pleasant excursion, but 'twas your grandfather's wish that I entreat them for help. If you agree to become my acolyte, you may accompany me. I shall send word to your tribe that I shall see to your care and training from this day forth."

Instead of showing fear or doubt, her expression filled with joy. "Oh, Master Flen, 'tis more than I dared ever hope."

Bhaltair gave her a benevolent smile. "Do you ken how to pledge yourself to me?"

"I do." She knelt down before him. "I vow to serve you, Bhaltair Flen. Ever at your side, always prepared to learn from you, so that I might do as the Gods will."

The pledge she spoke was not exactly correct, but she was young, and Bhaltair heard the deep emotion in every word. Not even Cailean, bless his heart, had sounded so fervent.

"There, now." He gently helped her up from the floor. "Let us break our fast together, and then we shall prepare for our journey."

Chapter Fourteen

L IVING WITH A hundred huge
warriors in a medieval stronghold,
Althea soon discovered, was a bit
like being a mouse in a maze filled with tigers.

At least the men were trying to be polite
about her presence. Most of the clan treated
her as if she were visiting royalty, bowing and
shifting out of her way whenever she came
near any of them. She definitely felt dwarfed
by every Skaraven, but it was their collective
silence that unnerved her much more than
their size. The clan did almost everything
without saying a word, and often employed
odd hand signals when they communicated
with each other. She guessed they had been

trained not to speak unless absolutely
necessary.

Then there was the fact that she was the
only female at Dun Mor. Whenever she joined
the clan in any area the awareness of her presence showed in an instant of stillness among
the men, as if she'd turned them to stone.
When they came near her, they behaved the
way a bomb squad officer would approach a
ticking suitcase left in a high-traffic area. Yet
she would swear that they weren't scared of
her—more like they were afraid of
themselves.

Given their behavior, Althea fully believed
that the Skaraven had been forbidden to
interact with any women. Yet she also
suspected that there was more behind the
bizarre taboo than Brennus had told her.

She'd expected to leave on the rescue
mission right away, until she learned that the
giants' encampment was on the other side of
Scotland.

"That can't be right," she told Brennus
after he showed her the location on a parchment map the shaman had drawn. "Ruadri
said you brought me back here the same night

I escaped. You couldn't carry me a hundred miles in a couple of hours."

"I didnae walk, my lady." The chieftain rolled up the map. "When the time comes to return there, I shall show you how we travelled."

"Will you also explain why your clan has almost nothing but the clothes on their backs?" She gestured around them. "Or how you could have built this stronghold when it's at least a thousand years old? Maybe you could also clarify the reason your tattoo— excuse me, your battle spirit—chose me, and exactly for what that would require the raven-shaped scars on my back."

He smiled a little. "You wouldnae believe it."

Talking to the chieftain always felt like trying to open a safe with the combination locked inside. "I believe that I was taken from the twenty-first century by giant immortals made of wood and a couple of mad druids, who dragged me through time seven hundred years for no reason whatsoever," Althea reminded him. "Go ahead, try me."

"You think I dinnae ken what you've

endured?" His expression grew remote. "'Tis no' so different than what I and my clan have borne. Aye, and more than you may ever fathom."

"Then tell me," she urged, moving closer to him. "I want to understand all of this, and I don't." She couldn't stop herself from reaching for his hand. "You can trust me with your secrets."

Brennus caught her wrist, watching her eyes as he bent his head to her hand. Althea thought he meant to kiss her palm, but he closed his eyes and breathed in.

"Here is one secret: I had a vision of you before we met," he said, his breath warming her flesh. "I saw you in the forest, gathering fern. I'd never beheld such loveliness as yours, Althea. 'Twas so bewitching that I couldnae move."

She touched his face. "I saw you too, or something like you. A shadow in the air." She dragged in a breath. "How can you do this to me when I'm so angry? All I want to do…but I can't. We can't." She stepped back to break the contact between them. "This isn't my time. I don't belong in it."

"Nor do the Skaraven," he said, stunning her.

Ruadri chose that moment to come in and ask Brennus to inspect some goods that had been brought to the great hall, and both men left her.

Althea decided to put her curiosity on the back burner. She saw for herself that the clan was stockpiling the weapons and supplies they would need for the rescue mission. She got her carryall back from the shaman, and was able to wear her own clothes again, although her garments made the clansmen stare at her even more.

For days Both Brennus and his War Master went over every detail she could recall of the giants' encampment. They'd even put together a rough layout of the farm using beans, rocks, twigs and moss to represent the people, buildings, forests, and what paths she remembered. Even so, she didn't know exactly where the camp was.

One night after the evening meal Althea joined Cadeyrn to go over the crude model again, which they'd set up on a table in the War Master's strategy room.

"I think it's as accurate as it's going to get."
She moved the white stone representing the
barn an inch to the left. "But I'm sure I'll
recognize the way when we're there." She
gazed thoughtfully at the barn. "While I was
there they kept two guards at the front, and
one at the back." She added three more beans.
"They've probably doubled the guard since I
escaped."

Cadeyrn moved to the opposite side and
looked at the rocks, pointing to a narrow
channel at the back of the barn. "If you'd run
in this direction, you'd have better concealed
your track."

She wondered if the War Master ever said
anything that wasn't a criticism or a veiled
accusation. "I'll remember that the next time
they take me."

"There willnae be a next time," he told
her. "If the *famhairean* take you again, they
shall kill you before the other females. You'd
be made to suffer much before you died, to
daunt the others from trying the same. 'Tis
their way."

"So, definitely don't get taken again,"

Althea said and suppressed a shudder. "Any other advice?"

"You may deny them their sport." He pulled a short dagger from his belt and offered the hilt to her. "Do you ken where to use it?"

For a moment she went blank, and then her throat tightened as she realized the only way she might escape death by *famhair*.

"In the heart, I imagine." Gingerly she took the blade, which felt cold and heavy in her grip. The reality of the fourteenth century hit her then, when suicide might be her best option. She met his gaze. "How can I be sure I won't simply wound myself?"

"If you've time, lodge the tip of the blade between the ribs, just below your heart, angle the blade, and fall forward onto the hilt. If no'"—he tapped the side of his neck—"thrust here."

As gruesome as his advice was, Althea knew the gruff man was trying to show her some kindness. "My thanks, War Master." As she tucked the blade inside her jacket, the scars on her back tingled, and she eyed the entry. "The chieftain is back from his night rounds."

A moment later Brennus stepped into the chamber. "Fair evening, my lady." He eyed Cadeyrn. "Manath needs your counsel on repairing the east flue."

"Aye, Chieftain. Fair evening, my lady." The War Master gave her a sharp look before he went out into the great hall.

Each night Brennus escorted Althea to her room on the underground level which adjoined his own chamber. She wasn't sure if the chieftain had arranged that because he wanted to be near her, or if he wanted to make sure she didn't take off again, but she didn't question it. The clan had installed a small but comfortable bed for her, and a primitive wash stand and basin so she could tidy up. Before she went to sleep, Brennus usually spent an hour sitting with her by his fireplace to share a hot drink and talk.

"Ferath brought this from Aviemore," the chieftain told her as he poured the steaming, brew he'd warmed over the flames. "'Tis made with blaeberries, hawthorn and sorrel."

Althea took a sip of the fragrant, sweetly tart concoction. "You should make Ferath your Tea Master." At his frown she said, "I forgot, you don't have that yet. Someday your descendants will love it almost as much as whiskey. Assuming you ever get over your fear of women, of course."

He dropped another log in the fire. "We dinnae fear females."

"Tell that to the clan that's been tiptoeing around me for the last week." Althea sat back and sighed. "I think I'm growing on your War Master, though. He gave me some, ah, helpful tips today."

"How to kill yourself if you're taken," Brennus said and sat down across from her. "You neednae carry the blade."

"I'm part of the rescue mission, so yes, I do." She saw his eyes shift away. "Oh, no. You're not tossing me in the *eagalsloc* again. I'm going with you."

"'Tis no' what I meant." He leaned forward, bracing his elbows on his knees. "You've but to use your power—on yourself."

She stared at him for a moment as she took his meaning. "All this confidence in me is so flattering."

"The raven doesnae choose the weak and

cowardly," Brennus told her. "That you bear the mark makes you as worthy as any of us."

She gave him a rueful look. "Then I'll try not to let down your battle spirit." She craned her neck trying to see her back. "I really wish you had some mirrors in this time, though, so I could get a look at this mark of mine."

"'Tis only your right," he agreed. But when she turned back to him his face seemed less sure than he'd sounded. Slowly he pointed to the rug in front of the hearth. "Kneel down with your back to me and I will show you."

Althea put aside her brew and got into position, wondering how this would work. She stiffened a little when he removed her jacket.

"Maybe you could just describe it to me," she suggested, feeling her hands begin to tremble.

"I shall," Brennus said quietly as he knelt down behind her. He tugged at the bottom of her shirt to free it from her jeans. "Unfasten your bodice."

Glancing down at her buttoned-up shirt, Althea saw the two peaks that her hardened nipples made through her bra and the fabric.

Being close to the chieftain always aroused her. His heat and scent had become like her own personal aphrodisiac. Even though he'd made it clear that they couldn't get involved, her hands shook as she opened her shirt up to her breasts. She left one button fastened over her bra.

"Okay," she said, her voice pitched too high.

His big hands slowly slid the back of her shirt up, folding it over her shoulders. It took him another minute to figure out how to unhook her bra. "Put your hands at your sides. Dinnae fret. 'Twill no' hurt."

She hadn't realize she'd been twisting her fingers together until she dropped her hands. Why couldn't she get over this attraction to him? She'd never had a problem freezing out men before Brennus.

Althea cleared her throat. "I'm ready. For the…whatever you're doing."

"'Tis the same mark as I bear," he said and shifted closer. "Here begins the raven's beak." His fingertip touched her left shoulder blade, and moved right over one of the sensitive spots. He traced a short, straight line, and then moved up in a curve. "The crown, and here the nape."

As he ran his finger over her scars and described the shapes, Althea closed her eyes to better imagine them. It didn't prove difficult, for his touch left in its wake nerves that seemed to be glowing under her skin. She could see the raven, and the primitive winged arrow behind it, exactly like the ink on his shoulder.

"You never told me why the raven marked me with your tattoo," she murmured, wrapping her arms around her waist as her belly filled with butterflies. "Is it because I got in its face when it was attacking you?"

"I cannae tell you." His hand trailed down to the small of her back before he took it away. "Marking a female with the skinwork of a male...if the Skaraven had been a Pritani tribe...but we arenae."

Althea turned to face him. "But you have Pritani blood, and your clan is your tribe."

He kept his gaze on her face. "You arenae Pritani, Althea."

"We don't know that for sure," she countered breathlessly. "I think my father's mother was Scottish. Her people could have been, way back when. I mean, now. So what would it mean if we were both Pritani, Brennus?"

"That my battle spirit chose you for me." His hands gripped the rug on either side of him. "As my mate. As my wife."

"So I'd be yours," she said, almost with a laugh, but it wasn't funny. "Just like that."

His voice went deep. "With my mark on your skin, no other Pritani male would touch you."

She reached for her shirt, but instead of closing it she undid the last button. Some wild part of her wanted him to look at her body, and she couldn't resist it. "So I'd have no choice?"

"You wouldnae want another." He leaned closer, his gaze locked on her mouth. "But I could never take you as wife. 'Twas always forbidden for me and my clan. The tribes bred us as warriors too hardened and dangerous to be trusted with females. Only males of the tribe came to our camp. Wherever we fought, the Pritani would hide their females from us."

Althea was shaken. It seemed horrific, and

yet explained so much about the chieftain and
his clan. "*None* of you have ever had lovers?"

"Of a kind," he said, sounding bitter now.
"We had pleasure lasses. Once we grew to
manhood the tribe's shaman brought barren
females to attend to our cocks every full moon.
He first chained us to our beds so that we
couldnae harm them. He forbade us to speak
or move during the ritual facking. To be sure,
he had men stand watch as the lasses mounted
us, and after we spilled to take them away.
'Twas part of our training, to control
our needs."

She watched him stand and turn his back
on her. "So you hated it," she said.

"Dinnae be daft," Brennus said, glaring at
the floor. "The Pritani kept us as warrior-
slaves. We ken naught but battle and hardship
and training for more. Only on the pleasure
nights did we ken any gentleness or joy. No' a
man among us could ever again look upon the
full moon, or hear the sound of chains
moving, without growing hard and ready."

"You don't have to be shackled to make
love to a woman," Althea said as she got up
and went to him. "You're not slaves anymore."

She touched his back. "I know you can be gentle. I'm not afraid of you."

"Battle and killing, 'tis all I ken, Althea." Looking tormented now, he nodded at her open shirt. "Cover yourself now, and go to bed."

"I don't fear you and I'll prove it." Shrugging out of her shirt, she peeled off her bra. "Look at me."

Brennus turned around, but as soon as he saw her naked torso he averted his gaze. "You arenae a pleasure lass."

"No, as it happens, I'm just a woman." She took a step closer. "I gave you your first kiss, didn't I? And despite this menacing warrior-slave reputation you've got, you didn't hurt me a bit." She pretended to think. "Plus you weren't in chains, I was. Maybe *you're* the one in danger now."

He made a rough sound. "You did stop two of the *famhairean.*" When she pressed against him, he didn't jerk away.

"You turned them into toothpicks. Please put your arms around me." She had to coax him to do that by dragging his hands up. "There. No blood spilled. You can hold me and not hurt me. I wonder what else you can do. We should check. Kissing, holding... touching would be next."

His shoulders went rigid. "Althea."

"It's just an experiment, Brennus." She moved back enough to create a gap between their bodies, and glanced down at her swollen, tight-peaked breasts. "I know where I'd like you to touch me. Maybe you can guess."

One of his hands left her back, and came up to rest on her shoulder. "'Twas never permitted."

"Now it is. I am giving you permission." She could see his eyes getting darker, if that were possible. "Touch me."

The hesitation with which he moved tore at her heart, but the brush of his fingers over the outer curve of her breast made her tremble. At first he stroked her so lightly she barely felt the contact. Then he circled her aureole with his thumb. Her nipple throbbed so hard in response she knew he could feel it.

"You've such softness." He watched his fingers, completely absorbed by the sight of his hand moving over her mound. "Your skin blushes for me."

The pinkness was spreading too. "That's because it feels good. Ah." The feel of him cupping her breast made her sway a little. "I thought about this when we kissed. How it would feel to have your hands on me."

"And I." He fondled her slowly, urging her closer with his other hand. "'Tis more to this experiment?"

He drew the word out, making even that sound sexy. "There's always more to learn." She drew his head down enough to brush her lips against his. "What do you want to do with me, Brennus?"

He muttered something under his breath, and then a loud knock hammered on the chamber door.

"Chieftain," Ruadri's voice called. "Taran and the herders are returned from Aviemore with urgent news. They await you in the great hall."

Althea felt like opening the door and socking the shaman in the nose. But she knew the chieftain had sent Taran to purchase enough horses for the clan, and urgent news usually meant it was bad.

"Damn it," she muttered.

Brennus touched his brow to hers, closing his eyes for a moment before he picked up her shirt and bra and put them in her hands. He held onto her fingers. "Another night, my lady."

Althea smiled and nodded, and then marched into her room to punch a few pillows.

Chapter Fifteen

B REAKING OUT OF their cold, miserable prison hadn't been Rowan's idea. After learning that Dr. Useless had set her up to be the distraction for *her* idiot escape attempt, she'd barely spoken a word to anyone but Perrin. But here she was, crawling out of the hole they'd somehow dug under one of the stall walls in the middle of the damn night.

As Lily crept to the edge of the barn to check the back, Emeline kept watch on the front. Perrin shook her head as Rowan tried to speak, and then made some kind of silly hand signal. The three women hurried around the barn and ran for the drying shed, leaving Rowan to stumble after them.

"Mind telling me what we're doing?" she demanded in a whisper.

Perrin rose just enough to peek over the shed's low roof. "We're leaving."

"With no supplies, no transportation, and no clue as to where we are?" When her sister didn't respond she sighed. "Look, they won't check the barn for another hour. We can go back, fill in the hole, and they'll never know."

The dancer gestured to Emeline, and pointed to a gap in the trees behind the farmhouse. "That's where they brought us in. I'm sure of it. It's wide enough to follow in the dark too."

The nurse glanced at Rowan before she murmured, "You're still pretty shaky, Perrin. We could wait another day."

Lily uttered a low hiss and gestured down with one hand.

Rowan flattened herself beside the other woman, and held her breath as one of the guards lumbered by the bush. The moonlight danced over the guard's scar-split face, making her let out a slow breath. Tri, the stupidest of the things that had snatched them, wouldn't notice an escape attempt even if they asked him for directions.

"Coig," the guard called out, and the sheep under his arm bleated and struggled piteously. "Fresh meat for you to carve."

Rowan felt Emeline stiffen beside her, and heard her make a choking sound. Grimly she clamped her hand over the nurse's mouth and watched until the guards moved out of earshot. Then she let go, and looked over the nurse's shuddering back at Perrin. "Snow White is about to have another pukefest. If the sound doesn't give us away, the smell will. We're going back. Now."

"You can if you want." Her sister touched Emeline's shoulder. "Deep, slow breaths, like last time. That's it, girl."

Rowan couldn't believe how oblivious they were. They really thought they were just going to run out of here without a single problem. "We are going to get caught. Perrin. Are you even listening to me?"

"We can't go back now," Lily said flatly. "You heard your sister last night. Althea is coming for us, and she's bringing help."

Rowan wanted to smack her alongside the

head, but the tough little blonde just might break her jaw. "Yeah, well, Perrin talks in her sleep. She has since we were in foster care. Tomorrow she'll probably tell you Santa is coming with eight tiny reindeer to rescue us." She looked toward the barn. "And Althea is dead."

"She's not, Ro," her sister told her as she helped Emeline to her feet. "She's alive and she's bringing help. We just have to hide until she gets here with them. But if you want to stay here to prove me wrong, be my guest. Come on, Lily."

Pride kept Rowan from chasing after them for all of two minutes. The moment she lost sight of her sister the old panic set in.

If you don't look after Perrin, young lady, someone will hurt her. She's far too reckless. Promise me you won't let her go off on her own. Ever.

She'd made that promise to their adoptive mother when Marion Thomas was on her death bed. A widowed piano teacher and a distant cousin of their birth parents, Marion had adored Perrin. She'd spent most of her savings to send her to Juilliard, while Rowan had to depend on patchwork scholarships and crap jobs to pay her way through trade school. Just after Perrin had graduated their mother had been diagnosed with stage four stomach cancer, and died only three months later.

Rowan didn't resent being the woodpecker to Perrin's swan. Anyone who saw her sister dance realized they were in the presence of greatness. But sometimes it felt as if her whole life would be spent keeping that damn promise to Marion.

This time Perrin was going to get them both killed, Rowan thought as she darted behind the farmhouse and into the trees. She had to trot to catch up with the other women, who were tiptoeing through the pine needles as if they were covering landmines, and halting to peer around every big trunk like Bigfoot was waiting.

"Since we're going to do this," she whispered to Lily, "could we maybe run our asses off now?"

"Emeline felt someone nearby," the blonde muttered back to her. "We're trying to see if they've got patrols—"

Two torches flared up directly in front of

them, revealing Murdina and Ochd barring the path.

The druidess made a scathing sound. "Foolish little wretches. Did you no' think we would take more precautions after the herbalist tried to escape? We ken the moment you broke the wards I cast about the barn. And to think I wished to teach you how to serve our cause." She scanned their faces. "The sickly one came through first, did she no'? Was this your scheme, then, wench?"

Nothing bad had ever happened to Perrin before. Everyone fell in love with her, so she'd never gotten beaten up at school or on the playground. And while she had the strong bones and physical stamina of a born dancer, she had never dealt with the kind of pain that Murdina and her thugs liked to inflict.

Rowan had.

"Seriously?" She stepped in front of Perrin. "I made her go first because she wanted to stay behind in the barn. She's nothing but a coward." She felt her sister clutch at the back of her shirt, but kept her sneer firmly in place. "This was all my idea."

More guards surrounded them as

Murdina smiled. "Ochd, take this one to the tethering post. Put the others where they might watch."

"No, you're wrong. She didn't do anything. *Rowan*." Perrin held onto her so tightly she tore out the back of her shirt as a guard dragged her away.

Ochd clamped a big hand on Rowan's shoulder as he marched her to the center of the yard between the farmhouse and the barn. "You shouldnae have defied the Wood Dream. Now you shall be punished."

"Story of my life, pal."

She couldn't understand why the guard kept talking to her. She'd told him fifteen different ways to drop dead, but he had some kind of thing for her. It was starting to get really creepy.

Rowan's belly clenched as she saw the tall, thick post that had been planted in the ground, and the large wooden cage sitting across from it. *This is going to be bad.* When the crazy druidess joined them she gave her a sunny grin. "So, what kind of punishment are we talking here, Teach? Time out? Paddling? Writing 'I will not try to escape' a couple hundred times? My handwriting really sucks, just so you know."

Murdina waited until the guards had stuffed the other women in the big cage before she faced Rowan. "For your treachery you shall receive fifty lashes. Ochd, hold the worthless slut in place."

The guard jerked her face-first against the post, pinning her arms around it. Rowan felt cold air rush across her back as the druidess tore away the rest of her shirt. Pressing her cheek against the rough wood, she looked at her sister, who had crawled to the front of the cage and had the bars in a white-knuckled grip.

"Just another beating," Rowan called to her. "No big deal." She jerked as white-hot fire scorched across her back, the pain of it so sudden and shocking that her lungs flattened. She hissed in a breath. "I got this. Snow White can give me a rub-down late—" The second lash sliced across her shoulders, taking some skin with it. "Later."

The first ten lashes schooled Rowan in all new elementary classes of pain. The next ten kicked her up to advanced courses in agony.

After that everything came in snapshots. Lily holding onto Perrin. Perrin beating her fists against the cage. Emeline's pale face going so white it looked like someone had dipped her in milk paint. Emeline keeling over into a limp lump.

Funny how they were all freaking out when she was the one being cut to pieces.

Rowan first braced herself against the post, and then stopped resisting. The whipping never stopped. Murdina didn't halt once to rest her arm or give herself a breather. The pain became an endless university of suffering, and she could taste her own blood as well as smell it. She didn't make a sound until she felt a feathery sensation over the raw expanse of her back. Was her skin starting to peel away from her spine? Did she even have any skin left?

Please, God, I'd like to die now. Really. Perrin'll be fine. Take me home I am so ready oh God please please.

"Rowan." Ochd shifted one of his hands to her mouth. "Bite down."

Another vicious lash made her wet face collide with his palm, out of which a small, leafy twig sprouted. He pushed it between her lips, and she caught it between her teeth. The taste of sap filled her mouth, mingling with the blood from where she'd bitten through her lip.

All that held her up after that were Ochd's hands and the twig between her teeth. Rowan barely felt the last ten lashes, but when they stopped she squinted at the cage through the cold sweat dripping into her eyes.

As she watched Rowan's face Lily cradled an unconscious Perrin in her arms. A small lump bulged from the dancer's brow. Emeline was back up and scraping some snow into a piece of cloth, which she carefully pressed over Perrin's lump. The dancer's eyelashes fluttered.

Lily met her gaze and gave her a thumb's up. Rowan managed a small nod before she collapsed to the ground.

Murdina hovered over her, her crazy eyes almost slumberous as she grabbed Rowan's arm and dragged her to the cage. Ochd released the door bars.

"You sadistic witch." Perrin lunged out at

Murdina, but Ochd backhanded her, flinging her to the back of the cage.

Murdina tossed Rowan into Emeline's arms. She hurt so much that she finally let out a whimper.

"That one." The druidess pointed at Lily, and the guard dragged the blonde out of the cage by her hair. He kicked the door shut, replaced the bars and then hauled Lily across the yard after Murdina. The three disappeared into the farmhouse.

"Don't touch her," she heard Emeline say. "Rowan, you've a great many welts on your back, but none of them broke the skin. I must make a compress for the pain."

That was when Rowan decided the nurse had gone crazy, because all she felt on her back was torn, agonizing raw flesh. She watched as Perrin lay on the cage floor beside her, and the site of her pretty face with the ugly lump almost made her smile.

"Your head?" Rowan managed to say.

"Lily hit me with a rock. No big deal." Perrin gently wiped away the tear-wash from Rowan's cheek. "You know I'm going to kill you after we get out of here."

"Uh-huh." Rowan felt Emeline lean over her with something that dripped cold on her ruined back, and decided to do the sensible thing and pass out first.

Her dreams replayed the whipping over and over. Sometimes Rowan split into two as the lashes cut her torso in half. Other times she watched herself being lashed, but there was no whip in Murdina's hand. She saw Ochd holding her, his cracked face resting on top of her head. The guard didn't look like a monster anymore. He looked like a lover. Like he loved her.

So, okay, Rowan thought sluggishly. *I'm in Hell now.*

The feel of the sun and the smell of fresh blood finally chased away the disturbing dreams. Rowan opened her eyes to see the nurse dabbing at Lily's battered face, and Perrin curled up and sleeping in one corner of the cage. She lifted her head cautiously, expecting to feel her back on fire, and felt only generally sore, as if she'd strained a few muscles.

"What did you put in that compress?" she asked as she slowly pushed herself upright.

She tried to look over her shoulder and then felt a damp clump fall away from her skin. It landed on the ground like a slush ball made of half-frozen pesto.

"Hendry gave me that poultice," Emeline told her. "He said it would heal most of the damage and, aye, that it did." The nurse tilted Lily's head to one side to examine her badly-bruised cheek. "If you feel better, I'd like to use some of it on our chef here."

"Yeah, sure," Rowan said. She scooped up the green stuff and handed it over. "Why'd they slap you around, Stover?"

"Hendry wanted to know why we tried to escape." The blonde shrugged. "I told him we were playing hide-and-seek with the guards, and the buggers cheated."

Chapter Sixteen

✤

THE MORNING AFTER Althea's interrupted interlude with Brennus she noticed that all of the men seemed on edge. Cadeyrn, who usually rose early, never showed up for the morning meal. Neither did the chieftain or his other clanmasters, except for Taran, who always seemed to be sitting alone in a corner somewhere for every meal. For the first time she realized why: the Horse Master watched everyone else while he ate.

She went into the section of the hall she'd mentally dubbed the great buffet, where the clan's cooks set out all the foods for their meals. For breakfast huge pots of soup and porridge sat steaming beside small mountains of berries and oatcakes. Another row of urns held water, pear juice and the clan's morning brew, which they made from a variety of herbs and spices.

Though she knew the clan was making preparations as fast as they could, she couldn't help but think of the other women and their meager rations. Soon enough their starvation would be over. She promised herself that.

"You again," Kelturan said, snapping her back to the moment. He supervised the clan's kitchen. "Do you never fill your belly, wench?"

Like the rest of the Skaraven he looked like a gladiator on steroids, but he had a deft touch with food, and an impressive knowledge of herbs. He also treated her with surly contempt, but only in front of the other Skaraven.

"Hey, I need regular feeding, or I get mean. You don't want to see me mean." She waited until the clansman getting his meal left. "Come on. Show me what you've got."

The cook went over to take a bowl out from a niche and handed it to her. "I reckon 'tis closer to what you demand. I didnae cook the oats so long today."

She and Kelturan had been secretly collaborating on making a medieval version of muesli for her morning meal, and when she sampled the cereal she smiled. "Aw, you added some honey. You *do* like me."

"I wouldnae feed that fodder to a horse." He looked around before he lowered his voice. "If it pleases you, my lady, I'll roast as much as you wish."

"You're a peach." She winked as she stole a handful of ripe blackberries to top the mixture, and then pretended to scowl as another clansman came in. "The abuse I have to take for a measly bowl of cereal." She turned on her heel and strode to the door.

"Then eat what the clan does," Kelturan shouted after her.

Althea suppressed a smile as she walked out into the hall. Curiosity about the news Taran had delivered last night drew her over to stand by his table. "Do you mind if I break my fast with you, Horse Master?" He didn't say yes or no, but he did get up to fetch a stool for her. "My thanks." Sitting with him felt a little awkward, as they'd never really spoken since her introduction to the clan. Unlike the rest of the Skaraven Taran had a lanky build, and blonde hair so light it sometimes looked white. "I was with Brennus last night when Ruadri came to tell him that you'd returned."

Taran nodded but kept watching the entry to the lower levels.

She'd have to go fishing, it seemed. "No luck buying horses?"

"No' enough for the clan." He turned to regard her, amusement in his cyan eyes. "You ask many questions."

"Yes, but you'll notice that I don't get many answers." She took a bit of her cereal and tried not to wish for milk again. "Maybe you could help me figure out something else. How long do you think it takes to ride a horse from here to where I was held?"

His brows rose. "Nineday. Twelve, if giving the mounts proper rest."

"So even on a horse, your chieftain couldn't have brought me back to Dun Mor from the giants' camp in a few hours. That's okay, don't do the I-cannae-say-my-lady thing." She offered him her bowl. "Want to try some? It's what we eat in the morning in my time."

Taran peered at the contents. "Willingly?"

"It's better with milk." She glanced around the room. "Do the Skaraven by any chance have a Cow Master with, say, more luck than you?"

That startled a husky laugh out of him. "'Tis too cold and rugged here for cows. We always traded for cheeses and beef with the dairies in the valleys. We couldnae keep milk long for spoilage."

"Raw milk is probably bad for me anyway." She put down her spoon. "What I really want to know is what urgent news you brought last night, because I'm nosy that way. But if that's cannae-say stuff I can keep talking about future food. Like sushi. That will probably horrify you too."

"'Tis no' a secret," Taran admitted. "Two druids came from the north to seek us. They have been asking after the clan in every village." He saw her expression and added, "No' the pair that took you. 'Twas an old man and a young lass."

Even hearing the word druid made the Skaraven collectively bristle, so Althea wondered if the pair had a death wish.

"They're the reason that the chieftain was out all night?"

"That, and other reasons, I reckon." His eyes shifted. "Now we may ken those."

She followed the direction of his gaze and saw Brennus emerge from the lower level stairs, followed by Ruadri. They both looked ready to punch something, which was not a good sign.

"I wouldnae," Taran said as she started to rise. "'Tis better no' to get between them now. They need to settle a dispute."

Her back grew almost uncomfortably hot. "With each other?"

"Aye." The Horse Master nodded at her bowl. "That you should keep in your lap now, my lady."

Without warning the clan got to their feet and began moving furniture until they cleared a large space in the center of the hall. Brennus and Ruadri stopped there and faced each other while the rest of the Skaraven gathered around them.

"Okay." Althea frowned. "Are we having another meeting?"

Taran coughed. "Ah, no, my lady."

"Flen can supply us with horses, clothing, food, tools, and what more the clan requires, Chieftain," Ruadri said, his voice rumbling across the hall. "All we need do is take it."

"You mean I need beg it from them. I'd rather fight on foot naked with my bare hands. I shallnae take a single boon from the tree-knowers." Brennus removed the dagger from his belt and tossed it to one of the watching men. "I am chieftain. 'Tis my choice."

Ruadri pulled off his cloak and a stone vial hanging from a cord around his neck. "I am shaman. 'Tis my duty to this clan. I challenge you."

Althea jumped as the two men slammed their hands together in a tight grip and squeezed until their arm muscles bulged.

"Oh, no," she whispered. "This is a very bad idea."

"Ruadri rarely challenges. 'Tis his size. He thinks it an unfair advantage." Taran leaned forward. "Never fear, my lady. 'Twill be good for them both."

The shaman swung Brennus around him and released his hand, sending the chieftain tumbling. He flipped over to land on his feet and lunged, catching Ruadri around the chest and slamming him to the floor.

Shouts of encouragement erupted from the watching men as the pair began punching each other. Althea winced at the heavy thud of every blow, and at one point covered her eyes with her hands to peek through her fingers. "Can't you make them stop?"

"'Tis a challenge. They fight until one prevails. They willnae kill each other," the Horse Master assured her. "'Tis more about settling serious matters in an amicable manner."

"Amicable? With their fists?" She winced as Brennus took a left hook to the jaw, and then clapped a hand over her mouth as the chieftain seized and threw a table at Ruadri. "You're sure they know not to kill each other?"

"Oh, aye. We cannae." As soon as he said that, Taran grimaced.

The fight went from nasty to brutal, and both men began to bleed. Anything they could throw at each other seemed to be fair game, and neither one seemed to be willing to retreat.

Part of a chair came flying at Althea,

which Taran calmly swatted away before it hit her. She grabbed her bowl and held it in her lap a few seconds before Brennus and Ruadri landed on the table in front of her, which collapsed under their combined weight with an ear-shattering crash.

Brennus glanced up at her. "My lady."

"Chieftain." She put a protective hand over her muesli.

"Your pardon," Ruadri gasped out, "my–" He grunted as the chieftain shoved him away from Althea.

"How long do these challenges take to settle?" she asked the Horse Master as she watched Brennus knock the shaman to the ground again.

"An hour. Mayhap two," Taran said, and then he stroked his jaw as the two men shot to their feet. "Unless they dinnae wish to prevail so soon. Then it can go on until they drop. No more than a day."

Althea thought of her parents, who hadn't gone a day without a screaming match over something. While her mother had often slapped or thrown things at her father, Will had never laid a hand on Sharan in anger. Yet even as a little girl Althea had known that the only thing that actually calmed them down was the noisy make-up sex they had after a fight.

Maybe that was why this brawl wasn't upsetting her as much as it should have. She'd spent half her childhood watching the Will and Sharan version.

Just as she was thinking of finding a bucket of cold water to empty on their heads, Ruadri and Brennus fell struggling to the floor, and the chieftain locked his arms around the shaman's upper torso. Leveraging his body, Brennus pinned Ruadri's shoulders to the floor.

The men fell silent, and when the shaman groaned "I concede" they cheered the chieftain's name.

Both men looked battered and bloody, and Brennus staggered a little as he got to his feet. He offered his hand to the shaman and helped him up before they nodded to each other and touched shoulders.

"And this is how you settle disagreements," Althea said to Taran. "Do you ever think about just talking to each other?"

He shrugged. "A fist says as much as a tongue, my lady."

"Ruadri has counseled that we should accept what the druids may offer the clan," Brennus said once the shouts died down. "In this he's right. I put my anger with the tree-knowers before the good of the Skaraven." He regarded the shaman. "I cannae look upon the old druid again, for I ken my temper shall be the end of him. You've my leave to parley with Flen."

Ruadri wiped some blood from his mouth. "I'll no' give him any advantage. The Skaraven live as free men now." He looked around at the clansmen. "So shall we be."

The Skaraven echoed his last words, and began cleaning up the mess from the fight.

"You may get your horses after all," Althea said and handed the rest of her muesli to Taran. "I'd better go offer some first aid."

"My lady," he called to her. When she looked back at him Taran nodded toward the chieftain. "'With Bren, 'tis no' the wounds you see that want healing. Go gently with him."

Althea cocked her head a little but nodded. She made her way across the hall only in time to see the chieftain take a torch and head down into the lower levels. She followed him to the deepest passage, where she grimaced as she skirted around the *eagalsloc*. Brennus went to the end of the tunnel opposite the room of carved stones, where he disappeared into a cloud of steam wafting from an archway.

Heat and dampness enveloped Althea as she walked in after him and stopped as Brennus's torchlight revealed an underground spring pool surrounded by low blocks chiseled in the stone.

She watched the chieftain sit down on one to remove his boots before she said, "That was quite a fight you had with Ruadri."

"'Twas but an angry tussle. Kanyth and I once fought for all of a day and half a night. 'Twould have been twoday if our trainers hadnae clouted us with cudgels." With painfully slow movements he pulled his tunic over his head. "At least Ruadri didnae fight me with his battle spirit. His moon can blind my raven."

Althea took in a quick breath. "You can do that?"

"Aye." Brennus eyed her. "Our ways seem barbarous to you."

"I wouldn't exactly call them civilized." As she saw him unlace the back of his trousers she turned her back on him. "Do you really think you should be taking a bath with all those cuts? The water down here might infect them."

He grunted, and then the sound of water splashing blended with his sigh. "We cannae grow sick anymore, my lady."

So he was finally ready to give her some answers. Althea decided she'd get as many as she could.

"Taran said you can't kill each other either. Your stronghold is a thousand years old. You carried me a hundred miles in one night. And you told me this isn't your time." She faced the pool to watch him swim toward her. "Did the druids bring you here from the past?"

"The Skaraven died in battle with the *famhairean* in the first century." He propped his arms on the edge of the pool. "The druids brought us back from our graves. They awakened us as immortals."

Two weeks ago, Althea would have suggested Brennus was delusional and in need of immediate therapy. All she'd witnessed and done since then, however, made his claim a little more plausible.

Because her knees shook like maracas, she sat down on one of the stone benches. "Would you tell me the rest, please?"

Brennus ducked under the water, and when he surfaced the wounds on his face began to shrink and heal. "Ruadri says we shall never age or ken sickness or disease. We can become as water, and he expects we'll use it to heal ourselves." He touched his shrinking woulds. "And 'tis so. It too permits us to travel great distances in but a few heartbeats. 'Tis how I brought you to Dun Mor, through the lochan to our river."

Althea looked at her hands. If she could have the power to freeze anything, then it wasn't a stretch to believe the Skaraven could turn into water. One thing still puzzled her. "If the druids did all that for you, then why do you hate them so much?"

Brennus's expression turned flinty. "The last time we fought the *famhairean* as mortals, we didnae reckon that the battle would end with our deaths. The druids did, but they said naught of it. They brought us back, aye, and bestowed eternal life on the clan, but only to protect them again. They might have awakened us any time, but they waited until the giants returned."

Knowing how they'd used the clan made her hate the rest of the druids too. "You didn't deserve that. I'm so sorry."

"'Twas long ago and cannae be undone. I've learned much from it." He looked up at her. "I dinnae wish you to return to your time, Althea, but I must let you go. To undo this thing forced on you."

She'd been so caught up in planning the rescue that she'd forgotten what would happen once they freed the other women. Brennus would take them to a sacred grove, where a portal would whisk them back to the twenty-first century. Even if he lived long enough to catch up with her in time, she knew he would never come looking for her. He was immortal, and she wasn't. They had no business knowing each other in her time or any other. He was just going to send her back, and she wanted to cry and plead and shout at him for even thinking it. But the worst part was that he was right.

"Anyway," she said tightly, "I'll...I'll see you later."

Hurrying out of the spring kept him from seeing the tears that had sprung into her eyes. It also kept her from saying something stupid, but Althea couldn't get it to stop repeating over and over in her head.

Don't undo it. Keep me here. I want to stay with you.

Chapter Seventeen

❧❧❧

L EAVING DUN MOR at dawn gave
Ruadri time to reach the agreed-on
meeting place an hour before Bhaltair Flen and his companion arrived. The
shaman found a sunlit rock on which to perch
and watch the road leading from the small
village where the druids had spent the night.

The spot proved popular. Birds fluttered in
the pines and birches around him, scolding
him with their piping voices. Their noise
roused a sleepy white and brown hare hiding
in the snow-patched dried grass, which went
still at the sight of the shaman before
bounding away.

He plucked a stalk of white heather from a
patch near his boot and lifted it to his nose.

According to Pritani legend, the rare color only grew where blood had not been shed. Tying it to a sword hilt was supposed to shield a warrior in battle.

Covering the world in white heather would not protect him, but he was not a warrior. He was a traitor.

Galan, the druid who had early on separated him from the other boys, had kept the truth from him for many years. In the beginning the spells and potions he'd taught him had been simply to treat injuries and sicknesses. Because Galan stood much taller and wider than the other druids Ruadri felt a kind of kinship with him.

That changed after Ruadri had been chosen by the moon battle spirit.

Galan began taking him into the mountains every sevenday to train as a warrior apart from the other boys. The first time had been the worst day of Ruadri's young life.

"I am a healer," he protested after the druid commanded him to battle bare-handed seven tribal warriors wielding blades and cudgels. "I dinnae wish to cause harm."

"Aye, but 'tis for you to prevent it." Galan

signaled the men, who came rushing at Ruadri. "Now fight for your life."

He assumed the druid was jesting, and cast a sleeping spell that caused the tribesmen to drop in their tracks.

"You cannae put an entire army to bed, lad, and you maynae have time to cast the full spell." Galan looked down at the slumbering men before he raised his hand, and another seven emerged from the trees. "Now use your battle spirit to repel them."

Ruadri had broken into a cold sweat. He knew exactly what his power could do. "No. I willnae."

The druid murmured under his breath, and suddenly Ruadri had no voice. Galan then gestured to the men, who spread out in a circle around the shaman. Then he pointed at Ruadri.

"Kill him."

Ruadri stared at his trainer, aghast at his order. Without his voice he couldn't use magic, and he carried no weapons. As the men closed in on him, Ruadri resigned himself to death.

White light filled his eyes as his arms blazed with the power of his battle spirit, which awoke and took over his will. A moment later it lifted his arms and slammed them together.

The skinwork on his forearms turned white-blue and joined to become a full sphere, which pulled in all the night from around them, making the air itself go dark. Blazing white light then shot out from the sphere in all directions, hitting the face of every warrior.

Each man dropped his weapons and fell to his knees to wail and claw at his eyes.

The light vanished, and Ruadri stared at Galan. He felt the spell silencing him dissipate.

"What did you do to me?" he demanded.

"Naught. The moon cannae be slain. 'Tis beyond this world, and owns you as much as the Pritani do." The druid pulled back the hood he'd used to cover his own face, and his dark eyes looked pitiless. "You will fight, lad, by blade or by spirit. 'Tis your choice."

There had been no choice, of course. The seven men he'd blinded never regained their sight. With shame and fury Ruadri had taken up the blade and learned to fight as well as any other Skaraven. He'd hated it, but he soon became one of the finest swordsmen among the clan.

When the Skaraven grew close to finishing their training Galan had come for Ruadri again. This time he took him to the sacred grove, where he spell-bound him and branded him with permanent body wards.

Then came the last, terrible truth.

"Why do you torture me?" Ruadri asked once the ritual was finished.

"You are my son," Galan said as he smeared a healing salve over his burned flesh. "'Twas decided by the conclave that a druid sire one of the Skaraven, to train the boy in our ways. For my size they chose me to mate with the largest and strongest female among the Pritani. We found love in our duty, but the work of delivering you killed her."

Ruadri had never wanted to use his moon power before that moment, but now he felt grateful that the druid had restrained him. "Why would you need a druid among the clan?"

"To prevent disaster," Galan said flatly. "The elders knew that the Skaraven would be unrivaled warriors. 'Twas feared that someday they might defy their masters and turn on the innocent. If that happened, every tribe in the land would fall beneath their swords."

That thought had never occurred to him, but then he didn't have a spider's web for a mind. "You're mad. My brothers would never—"

"They arenae your brothers," Galan said softly. "You are druid kind, Ruadri. You owe your loyalty to us. 'Tis now your sacred duty to stand watch over these killers. If the Skaraven choose to rebel, you shall inform us. If there isnae time, you shall stop them."

Ruadri hated Galan's callous scheme, and now knowing they were blood-kin made him feel sick. But as repulsive as the druid's aims were, he knew better than Galan just how dangerous the Skaraven were. The clan could very well turn on the innocent, and there would be little the Pritani could do to stop them.

"I trust my clan," he said finally. "They willnae betray the tribes."

"I dinnae care what you think." He drew a blade and held it under Ruadri's chin. "Swear to me that you shall serve as Watcher, my son, or I'll end you here and—"

"Then do it," Ruadri said through his teeth. "You may be my sire, but I'm no' a traitor."

Galan leaned closer. "When you are dead, I shall go to the training camp and poison their food and water. No one will ken why they suffer, until 'tis too late to save them."

It was almost worth it to die so that he might reincarnate and return to slit his sire's throat. His life no longer mattered to him, not after learning he had been born to betray. Yet to know that his death would send his brothers to theirs would torment him for eternity.

"If I am granted one request, I shall be your Watcher." He met his father's gaze, and for the first time realized they had the same eyes. "Never do I want to lay eyes on you again."

"So, we share my fondest wish since the moment of your birth." Galan gave him a cold smile. "Agreed. Report every new moon to Bhaltair Flen." He released the spell bindings and walked out of the grove.

In that, the druid had kept his word. After

that night Ruadri had never again seen
his sire.

The sound of ponies drew him back to the
present, and he crushed the white heather in
his fist as he saw the druids approaching.
Standing and walking down to the village road
gave him time to clear his thoughts, although
when Bhaltair hailed him he felt the ink on his
arms move.

Ruadri clenched his fists and drew in a
deep breath before he greeted the old man as
civilly as he could. "Fair day, Master Flen."

"'Tis good to see you, Ruadri lad," Bhaltair said. The old man waited for his young
companion to dismount and accepted her help
climbing down from his mount. "We've much
to discuss. Forgive me, this is Oriana Embry,
my new acolyte. My dear one, this is the Skaraven Shaman, Ruadri."

The lass bobbed nervously. "'Tis a pleasure, Shaman." She looked fearfully at the
old druid. "Might I water the horses,
Master?"

"Aye, do." As she led them off, Bhaltair
hobbled over to the rock, and sat down with a
wince. "The journey has bedeviled my bad

leg, but it cannae be helped. How fares the clan since your return to your stronghold?"

Ruadri tonelessly informed him of their restoration of Dun Mor, and Brennus's rescue of Althea Jarden. "The chieftain plans to return to the *famhairean's* encampment and free the other four females, if they still live. We are purchasing what we may, but we need a hundred battle-trained horses, food, tools, and more clothing enough for the clan."

"Suggest to your chieftain that he call on Clan McAra in the midlands," Bhaltair advised. "They breed the finest mounts in the highlands, and their tribe never paid the debt they owed the Skaraven. For the rest I've arranged caches to be left for you at these spots on your borders." He took out a scroll and unrolled it to show him the marked areas. "Will your clan confront the *famhairean*?"

"We go to take back the females," Ruadri said. "Naught more." He took the scroll and tucked it under his chest strap.

"They havenae stopped killing. They murdered my oldest friend, Gwyn Embry," Bhaltair said and nodded toward Oriana. "Her grandfather. Nor did he go quickly. They stole him from his settlement and tortured him for days."

Ruadri frowned. "How did the grand-daughter escape?"

"The tribe wasnae attacked, but they have taken refuge in the lowlands. Oriana came to me." The old man went still. "By the Gods. They took Gwyn from his settlement but killed only him."

"Every druid settlement the *famhairean* found they always destroyed, just after they slew the entire tribe. They didnae take your friend by chance. They wished to find you through him." He nodded at the young druidess, who was leading the horses back to them. "Do you reckon they followed her?"

"No. She used the groves. Say naught of this." Bhaltair mopped some sweat from his brow and forced a smile for Oriana. "My dear one, would you take our mounts across the road to that meadow there? We'll let them graze a wee bit before we ride back."

The young druidess gave Ruadri another timid look before she guided the ponies away.

Once the lass was out of earshot, Bhaltair

said, "'Tis why they tormented poor Gwyn so long and brutally. To punish me."

"They desire more than mere grief from you, Master Flen." The shaman almost felt sorry for the old man. "'Twas your magic that defeated and imprisoned them. If your friend had told them how to find you, you and your people would be now dead. He suffered because he kept his silence. Unhappily, others maynae do the same."

"I must go into hiding with my tribe," the old druid said and peered around them. "'Tis but two leagues to the nearest grove. I shall take Oriana there so we may return to my settlement at once." He paused before he said carefully, "Shaman, you ken that we shall never be safe again until the quislings and the giants are defeated. No mortal or druid shall."

"Mayhap we should move the Dawn Fire to the Skaraven stronghold, Master." Oriana stood not a yard away, her small hands folded in front of her. "They're the mightiest of warriors, and can well protect us."

Ruadri said "We cannae" at the same time Bhaltair said "No, lass."

The druidess's eyes gleamed with tears.

"'Tis hopeless, then, for the *famhairean* will find the tribe, just as they did my grandfather. Master, please, can you no' persuade the shaman to help us?"

"'Tis one place they can never enter," Ruadri said, although his idea soured his belly and spread a bitter taste on his tongue. "My sire, Galan, once dwelled in the eastern woodlands. His tribe may yet still."

"Aye, they do," the old druid said. "What of it?"

"When Galan was teaching me to cast protective spells over land, he said that his tribe thwarted attack by warding the land from underground with spell stones. They left only one way to enter and leave the woodlands safely."

Bhaltair thought for a moment. "I remember him teaching you. 'Twas a water trick, by walking in where no man would walk."

"Through a crooked river to the west, where the white water begins. The rapids and waterfall there are but an illusion." He pushed the memory of his sire out of his mind. "When you take your tribe in, they shall know you to be a friend of their blood-kin and give you sanctuary."

"Oriana, fetch our mounts." The old druid rose and swayed for a moment before he planted his cane. To Ruadri he said, "I'll return here once I've settled my tribe and the lass with your sire's kin. No, dinnae argue it. I've vowed to put things right with the Skaraven." He sniffed. "I may be old, and hobbled, but I'm no' ready for the well. Nor will I hide from the *famhairean*."

Ruadri accompanied him to the pony, and tactfully helped Bhaltair mount. "Think on it again, Master Flen. I cannae promise my clan shall stay here. After we return Althea and the others to the future, the Skaraven may leave Caledonia forever."

"'Tis called Scotland now, lad," Bhaltair reminded him. "We'll see what we see when we see it. Until then, keep watch, and meet me here in sevenday. We cannae wait for the next new moon."

Chapter Eighteen

THE DAY AFTER the brawl Althea decided to avoid Brennus. Since he was seeing to the final preparations for the rescue mission, she wasn't too worried about running into him. But after the temptations simmering silently between them had nearly erupted, she needed to stay occupied. She spent the day helping Kelturan pick through and sort the sacks of berries, roots and herbs brought in by the clan's foragers.

"What are you going to do with all these green juniper berries?" she asked as she lugged another bucket to the kitchen's enormous stone-slab work table. "You can't eat them raw, unless you like horribly bitter fruit.

Which, given your personality, would not surprise me."

"I thought to add them to your morning fodder." When she glared at him, he took a handful of the berries and pressed them between his palms. A sharp, resinous smell spilled into the air. "The green we crush and strew in the lower passages and chambers, to sweeten the air. Mayhap I should stuff your ticking with them."

"Berry air freshener. Very clever. Don't you touch my bed." She nodded and then gestured toward the mature, purple variety. "What about those?"

"I crush and stuff them into boar before roasting, so they may flavor the meat." His expression became almost dreamy. "'Tis naught better. Well, mayhap frog, but the hunters never catch enough for a meal. I'll catch one for you to sample."

"A frog snack. Yum." She swallowed hard. "You know, I might be allergic. I'll stick to boar."

He made a rude sound. "You've never been starved. Frog looks grand to a lad's shriveled belly."

Her smile slipped a little, and she turned away to fetch another sack. The Skaraven might be huge, scary warriors, but they hadn't been born that way. As boys they had been trained and treated like livestock instead of children, and now she was learning sometimes they endured even worse. Being forced to fight every day must have been awful, but why subject growing boys to deliberate starvation?

Althea knew she was over-reacting, and why. Until her parents had dumped her on her uncle, she'd been starved of a lot of things: love, nurturing, understanding, acceptance —and food.

"You're a tetchy wench," Kelturan said when she brought a bundle of sorrel to the table. "If I spoke out of turn, you might remember I'm a man and no' freeborn."

"No one is born to be a slave, Kel." She dropped the sorrel and turned to him. "Actually I starved quite a bit when I was a little girl. Mostly because my mother forgot to feed me, but sometimes because my parents fighting scared me so much that I couldn't swallow. Fortunately, I got away from them, and my uncle raised me on his farm. He loved me, at least until he died of an infection that ate him. Literally." She swiped at her eyes. "I'm sorry. I don't know where all that came from."

He gave her a long, silent look before he said, "Your heart. I think you starve it now."

"That's...probably true." Feeling deeply shaken, Althea put on her brave face. "So, what do I do about it? Not that I'm going to eat a frog stuffed with anything, you understand."

The cook tossed her one of the small, hard apples he kept hoarded away somewhere. "Forget your fear, my lady, and feast. And try frog. 'Tis much like rooster."

Althea smiled and took a bite of the tart fruit before she went back to work.

When it came time to prepare the evening meal, Kelturan chased her out of the kitchen, claiming the other cooks would burn the food while gaping at her. Since he was probably right about that, Althea went out into the great hall to find something else to do. There she found Cadeyrn and a group of the clan's carpenters putting the final touches on what looked like the world's biggest picnic table.

"Wow." She joined the War Master to survey the impressive project. Wide, fresh-sawn oak planks supported by rows of short tree stumps had been fitted together by wedge-shaped dovetailing at the ends. Whoever had finished the wood had rounded the straight edges and polished the top surface to smooth perfection. "This is really nice. What is it for?"

"Eating meals." Cadeyrn gestured for the carpenters to carry over sections of shorter planked stumps, which they placed like benches on either side of the table. "'Twill seat the entire clan, although the patrols and sentries on duty cannae join us. What made you weep?"

She wiped a stray tear from her lashes. Even when he was busy, the War Master never missed anything. "Some bad old memories. Some really good advice. You know. Life."

"Once Taran secures the mounts we need, we'll have all we need to free the others." Cadeyrn gave her a shrewd look. "Then you shall go home, my lady."

That almost sounded like a question. "Yes, I will. I have to. I have my research, and well, my research." She thought of the ferns she had been collecting, and all her hopes for finding new treatments for incurable infections. Since she'd come to the fourteenth century she hadn't thought about it once. "I really loved my work."

"'Tis a noble thing you do, finding herbs to make potions for the sick." He glanced at her. "If 'tis what you still wish."

She saw the chieftain come in the front entry with Taran, followed by a bunch of clansmen carrying big bundles. "Excuse me."

Althea couldn't leave the stronghold without an escort—Brennus's orders—but she had complete access to the keepe and the lower levels. She slipped into the hall that led to the forge, where she had watched Kanyth hammering out new swords for the men. He was nowhere around, however, and after she admired the rows of shiny blades he'd made, she lit a torch and wandered to the back stairs. Holding the flame in front of her, she walked down until she reached the spring level.

Althea wasn't sure why she went directly to the carved stone room, but the moment she stepped inside the scars on her back seemed to thrum. Carefully she tucked the torch in a bracket before she made her way through the slabs to the black crystal raven stone.

Dark, menacing and beautiful, Althea thought as she stood before the carved morion. *Just like him.*

"I'm not sure how this works, but here goes," she said, and dropped down on one knee. "I've got a raven on my back. Not the one you put there, the other one. I know he's the chieftain, and I'm just the annoying house guest. Seriously, I know we've both got jobs to do. Mine is waiting for me in the future. I don't belong here, but he does. These men need him. This world needs him but…so do I."

The room remained still and silent, but Althea's back rippled with a sweeping warmth that made her sigh.

"Brennus and I…" She paused but then plunged on. "All we've got is right now. Maybe a couple more days." She took a deep breath. "I don't want to starve anymore. I want the feast. I can't be his mate, or his wife, but for as long as we're together I can be his. If that's enough, if that's what I should do, please let me know. Send me a raven."

A sound echoed in the outer passage, making Althea jump to her feet. A long, wide shadow stretched into the chamber, and then Brennus appeared in the doorway.

"My lady." He smiled a little. "Will you come and share the evening meal with us?"

And then she knew. "Sure. I'm starving."

Up in the great hall the clan had gathered around Cadeyrn's new table, which was covered with platters and bowls of food from Kelturan's kitchen. Big oval trenchers made of dark bread served as plates, and while there were no utensils nearly every man in the clan had new daggers, which they used to pick up and slice the meat from the platters.

"Where is Kanyth?" Althea asked as the chieftain guided her to sit by him at the head of the table.

"I sent him to bed," Brennus told her as he filled her goblet with an amber beverage. "He's been awake for threeday working in the forge, and his hands need rest."

Althea tried the drink, which was a very sweet fruit cider, and then tried to focus on the food the men passed around the table. Nothing interested her as much as the chieftain, however, so she nibbled and sipped while she watched him eat.

Brennus usually put away enough food to fill three other men, but he didn't seem very interested in the roast boar, either. Instead he listened to the men talking about the lakes and rivers they'd been using to travel to distant towns and villages, and how building a new smokehouse would allow them to preserve the bountiful game the hunters had been bringing in every day.

Finally the meal came to an end, and like the rest of the clan Althea cleared her place and drained her goblet.

"I've something for you," Brennus said, as he helped her to her feet. "Come and see."

Althea's heart hopped like a kangaroo in the bush as she walked with the chieftain to his chamber. She'd settled her own conflicting feelings and had gotten the all-clear from the raven spirit. Since Brennus had never been with a woman without being chained, he'd be nervous, maybe even frightened. No matter how excited she got she'd have to go slow and be gentle with him.

Inside the chamber Brennus added a split log to the fireplace and lit some candles Althea hadn't before seen. The scent of warm honey and beeswax spread through the air, blending with the heat from the hearth. They must have come from the hive the hunters had found. The clan never wasted anything.

She, on the other hand, had wasted too much time.

"Ruadri and Taran went to the midlands this morning to buy horses from the Clan McAra," Brennus said as he brought a large bundle wrapped in new linen and put in on his chair. "They have more than even we need, but the laird refused to sell a single mount to them."

She wondered why he was fiddling with the bundle when he could be putting his hands on her. "Why not?"

"The McAra told Ruadri that he must first meet the clan's chieftain and his lady wife." Brennus took a long, shining length of silver-embroidered emerald fabric from the bundle and shook it out. "I had this fetched from a trading ship."

Althea looked at the gorgeous gown, which had intricate stitching over yards of fine silk, and an over skirt of white lace so thin it looked like mist. She'd never seen a more beautiful garment, and it made her so angry she wanted to slap him.

This was what he had for her. A dress.

"It's very pretty," she told him. "So who's going to wear it and pretend to be your lady wife? It might fit Taran, but it'll be a little short, and with those shoulders he'll probably rip the sleeve seams. Or maybe you can send him to hire a village woman willing to act the part. Because there's no substitute for a real medieval woman, is there?"

"'Tis meant for you." Brennus draped the gown over his chair. "You're angry with me."

"No, Chieftain, this is more like furious." She didn't get to the chamber door before he did, however. "Step aside. I'm sleeping somewhere else tonight."

Brennus reached behind his back and dropped the bolt bar on the door. "First explain this to me."

A short laugh escaped her. "You want me to dress up and pretend to be your lady. Your wife. Just to get horses for the clan, so we can rescue the others, and I can go back with them to my time. You really can't wait to get rid of me, can you?"

"You cannae stay," he countered. "You told me yourself."

"That's the plan." She went over, grabbed the gown and nearly hurled it into the fireplace. But that was what Sharan would have done, and she wasn't her mother. Carefully she folded the voluminous dress and placed it back in the linen wrapping. "Unfortunately, I'm not your wife, Brennus. I'm not your lady. You've made it clear that I'm never going to be, so I really don't think I can act the part." The sound of metal clinking made her look back at him.

Brennus took a pair of shackles from under the pillow on his bed. He looked down at them for a long time, and then wordlessly held them out to her.

Althea marched over to him, snatching the cuffs and chain and throwing them across the room. They crashed into the wall and shattered, falling in icy chunks to the floor.

"I'm not a pleasure lass, either," she told him as she moved to the end of the bed and took off her jacket. Stepping out of her sneakers, she said, "You want me, fine. You're going to have to deal with a real woman." She jerked her shirt over her head, and unfastened her jeans, shoving them down until she could kick them off with her socks. "No chains, no ritual facking, no relieving of needs. Just you and me, making–" Big hands grabbed her and tossed her face-down on the bed. "Love."

Brennus flipped her over, pinning her under him with his body as he tore off her bra and ripped away her panties. He dragged her wrists up above her head. "You would be my woman?"

Althea had never seen such dark torment in his eyes. All her anger melted away. "I am yours, Bren. I have been for a while now. Maybe since the first time you kissed me."

He buried his face in her hair, his body shaking over hers. Slowly he turned his head, gliding his mouth over the curve of her ear and along her jaw. He kissed the corner of her lips, and then covered her mouth with his.

Althea met his tongue with hers, tasting heat and man, and groaned as he took her mouth. He kissed her with shattering passion, hungry and demanding, nothing held back, everything she wanted. She felt her breasts swell and her thighs knot as an unbearable need consumed her, unlike anything she'd ever felt. Wrapping her legs around his, she lifted her hips to rub herself against the thick ridge of his erection.

Brennus released her wrists and pushed himself up on his knees to yank off his tunic. The sight of his wide, hard chest made her reach out so she could feel all that glorious muscle under her hands. The moment she touched his ink the scars on her back began to pulse with a delicious sensation, as if they were being caressed.

He moved off the bed to strip the rest of his clothes, and then he stood looking down at her. The long, thick column of his penis had grown so erect it throbbed against his lower belly, and for a moment she wondered if she'd taken on more than she could handle. It had been over a year since the last time she'd made love. But this was Brennus, and he was magnificent, and her body was so ready for him her inner thighs were already slick. Althea stretched, parting her legs as she turned toward him.

"Come here," she said, holding out her hand. When he took it, she drew him back to her, cradling his hips with her thighs and pressing her breasts against his tightly-pebbled nipples. She waited for him to move, and when he didn't she said, "You can do anything you want. Touch any part of me you'd like."

He placed his hand over her breast, and his fingers trembled. "I'd put my mouth on you."

She tucked her hand around his neck and guided his lips to her nipple. He pressed a kiss there before he took her in his mouth, laving her with his tongue before he sucked on her.

The pull of his mouth made the throbbing need grow intense, and she gripped his hair, pushing her breast against his lips so he'd take more. "Yes, like that. Oh, that's so good."

He released her nipple with a soft pop and moved to suck at her other breast. His arm slid under her, lifting her shoulders from the bed to drape her over his forearm. His fingers rubbed her wet peak and trailed down over the lower curve of her breast. His palm slid along her hip, where he kneaded her soft flesh, but he didn't move lower.

He was still chained by the past, Althea thought, and gripped his hand to guide it to her thigh. "Try here." She parted her legs wider. "You might like it. It's a fun place."

Brennus watched her face as he moved his hand higher. His fingers moved over her, exploring her folds and the slickness of her arousal. When he grazed her distended clit she couldn't help moaning, and he returned his fingers to caress the hard little knot.

"'Tis this wee gem that brings you to bliss," he murmured.

The way he touched her was making her crazy now. "I might just get there without it."

He pressed his thumb over the nub, circling it gently. "I'd kiss you here until you beg me stop, but more I want to come into you."

"We've got all night," she promised. "And I really want you inside me too."

Brennus shifted her onto her back, nestling between her thighs. His hand shook as he guided the swollen dome of his cockhead to her, fitting it in place before he braced himself over her. "Althea. My woman."

"Yours." She rolled her hips to lodge him deeper. "Now take me, please."

He sank into her, one slow inch at a time, his big body so tense every muscle bulged from the strain. At the same time his eyelids drooped, and his lips parted, his expression that of a man discovering an ecstasy he'd never known.

"Your quim is so soft and tight on me." His chest heaved as his balls pressed against her, his shaft engulfed by her to the root. "Fack, I'll spill if I move."

The tight, hot stretching of her pussy around him had Althea panting. "Look at me, Bren." When he did she gripped his cock from within, tightening and easing as she massaged his length. "Feel that? That's you and me. That's all that matters."

Her words broke the last of Brennus's chains, and he pressed her down, his hands gripping her shoulders as he drew back and thrust deep inside her. She cried out as the brutal stroke sent a flood of sensations pouring through her belly and breasts, and then he was plunging back again, over and over as he fucked her.

His mouth grazed hers before he tucked his hot face against her neck, his hand taking her breast and roughly caressing it in time with his strokes.

The slap of their slick skins and the scent of sex pushed Althea to the edge of climax, but she held back. She wanted to feel him jet into her as she came, to take his seed with her into that soul-rending explosion of delight. He'd always be her first that way, the only man to bring her such a joy.

All of the candles in the room went dark as a brilliant light glowed around them. Althea saw his tattoo glowing an electric blue, and somehow knew the same bewildering illumination was coming from her scars. Excitement swelled impossibly huge inside her as the light coalesced into a shower of sparks that ran over their bodies.

Brennus made a rough sound, and his cock worked inside her with heavier, harder thrusts. He lifted his head to look into her dazzled eyes, his own reflecting the sparks dancing over them. "For you, my lady."

He flung his head back as he came, his shaft swelling and jerking inside her. Althea clamped around him one last time and felt her own pleasure spin out of control and burst. She lost herself as her climax whirled around the spurts of his cream, taking them both in a maelstrom of rapture.

When Althea finally came back to earth Brennus had shifted onto his side and held her as if he never intended to let her go again. Inside her body she could feel his shaft, still hard and ready to give her more. His hand stroked her hip with a slow possessiveness that made her smile.

"I guess I could wear the dress now." She wrinkled her nose at him. "Unless you have some reason to keep me naked and in this bed."

He tipped up her chin and gave her such a tender kiss that she shivered with new delight.

"You ken what you've done for me, my lady. Anything you desire is yours." His mouth hitched. "But I dinnae reckon Taran will wear it."

"Okay," she said. He was only asking her to play a part, but it would give her a little to dream about when she did go back to her time. "When do we go meet the McAra?"

"On the morrow." He tugged her leg up over his hip and gripped her bottom as he pushed deeper inside her. "Now, on that reason to keep you here."

Chapter Nineteen

✦❦✦

WAKING FROM A deep, dreamless sleep, Brennus felt an unfamiliar weight wedged against his shoulder. He didn't have to open his eyes to know it was Althea, sleeping beside him. He lay quietly for a time, listening to her breathe and feeling her skin warming his. The scent of her had changed since last night. He could smell himself on her now. That, too, gave him no small pleasure.

At last he looked upon her, tucked beneath his arm, her cheek pressed to his skinwork. Her flame-red hair, rumpled by his hands, lay in a soft, bright cloud around her pretty face. He'd never seen a woman look so contented, but then all he knew of women were pleasure lasses. They'd been solemn, as befitted their task, performing a necessary duty with the Pritani's most dangerous beasts. Some had been fearful, others gripped by lust, but all of them had looked upon Brennus without a flicker of affection or kindness.

Now Althea slept beside him, as trusting as a wife with her husband. As if he were no more than an ordinary warrior, abed with his lady.

The Chieftain of the Skaraven would never be ordinary or a husband. But as a man Brennus yearned for that now, if only to have that simple life with her. To protect and care for her. To take her to bed every night, to love her and wake every morning like this. To watch her belly swell with his bairns, and then to see her suckle them at her breast. To raise their sons and daughters and grow old together. To lay beside her in the ground, together even after death. That might have been their life, had he and Althea been born to this time. Just a man and woman, destined to meet and to love.

The raven on his shoulder turned its head

and looked upon Althea. Its eyes glittered as it then beheld Brennus.

You've a second life, the clan, and freedom, a scratchy voice said from within. *'Twill be as you shall have it, Chieftain. Yet you remain bound to what you've been. Did your mate teach you naught?*

Brennus carefully eased away from Althea, and silently rose to dress. His skinwork stung like nettles on torn flesh, but the pain was nothing compared to his own shame. He looked back at his lady for a long moment before he left his chamber and made his way to the great hall.

Every member of the clan stood waiting for him, their eyes narrowed and their bodies stiff. Cadeyrn would not meet his gaze, nor Ruadri, who clutched the stone vial he wore around his neck.

"Fair morning, Chieftain," Taran greeted him, his expression resigned.

"My baws 'tis fair." Kanyth came forward, his hands wrapped in crusted bandages. "Threeday I work without rest, and you send the raven to wake me? For what? To take up the hammer with my teeth?"

"Your spirit drove every one of us from

our beds, Chieftain," Cadeyrn said stiffly. "No'
even the sentries and patrols couldnae remain
on duty. The raven compelled us to assemble
and wait on you." He sounded tired and
angry. "What does it want?"

Brennus picked up a bucket of water from
the hearth and dropped it on the long table.
He then took his half-brother by the arm and
dragged him over to it.

"We yet live as warrior-slaves. We hide
from the world in Dun Mor. We hate those
who bred, trained and betrayed us. We turn
our backs on the innocent, and their suffering.
We've become cowards." He thrust Kanyth's
hands into the water.

The Weapons Master howled, and then
went completely still. He raised his hands and
tore away the dripping bandages, revealing
them to be whole and unmarked. "Fack me.
What magic is this?"

"'Tis yours, Ka. Water heals our wounds
now and takes us wherever we wish to journey.
We cannae age or sicken or die easily. The
Skaraven shall never again suffer as we once
did. And what do we with these grand gifts?"

Brennus dumped the water on the floor. "Naught."

The Weapons Master flexed his hands. "Now that you've shown me the water healing, I'll be glad to use the bucket."

"'Tis no' about that," Cadeyrn said and came to stand before Brennus. "Ruadri parleyed many gifts and goods from the tree-knowers. Mayhap some were bespelled to bring their old warrior-slaves to heel."

"You ken that the druids cannae control our battle spirits," Brennus countered. "'Tis our power, no' theirs. As for bringing us to heel, we've done that for them. Free men dinnae cower and hide from evil. They fight it."

The clansman all looked at each other, their expressions filled with anger, but their eyes dark with shame.

"The Skaraven have been made immortal so that we might live as *we* choose. 'Tis time we become free men in truth, and take wives, and build a new life for the clan. Last night my lady agreed to play my wife for the McAra." He looked up as a shadow stretched out over the clan, taking on the shape of a giant raven. "I dinnae want Althea to pretend it. She's my woman, and if she'll have me, I shall marry her."

"Shouldn't you be proposing to me?" a wry, sweet voice asked.

Brennus turned to see his lady, resplendent in the emerald gown, walking toward him. She had put up her hair in woven braids that gleamed like a fiery crown. "I didnae wish to wake you."

"That's okay." She hunched her shoulders. "The raven did."

"My Gods," Kanyth muttered. "If we can take wives half as lovely, I'll fight evil." He yelped as Cadeyrn smacked the back of his head. "I cannae help it. Look at her. She's a facking princess."

"Scientist," Althea drily corrected him. "But I do clean up nicely." She regarded Brennus as she came to his side and tucked her hand in his.

The raven soared down to perch on Brennus's arm and spread its wings over him and Althea. It shimmered with blue light before it dissolved away.

"With freedom comes obligation," the

chieftain said. "'Tis for us to fight the evil that has come to destroy our world, for as immortals only we have the power to defeat them. 'Tis the path I choose." He met Cadeyrn's scowling gaze. "No' for the sake of druid kind. I fight for my lady and the others being held. For the mortals the *famhairean* intend to slaughter. To honor all those who have died at their hands." He scanned the faces around him. "Will you fight with me?"

Taran dropped to his knee. *"Bràithrean an fhithich,"* he said, his quiet voice booming through the silent hall.

All around him the Skaraven began to kneel, echoing the battle cry. Kanyth grinned like a boy at Althea as he joined them. Soon every man in the hall knelt before Brennus, except Cadeyrn, who stood looking at Althea, and Ruadri.

Brennus knew he'd never prevail over the giants without his second or his shaman. "Brothers?"

"If 'tis your wish," Ruadri said as he lumbered forward and knelt before him. "I fight with my chieftain."

The War Master followed suit, but when

he looked up he again inspected Althea. Then he met Brennus's gaze, and his own turned cold. "I fight with my brothers. As we yet need horses, I will go and prepare for our journey to the midlands." He stood up and leaned close to say just for his ears, "Only ken this. If you forget yourself, even once, I shall gut you." He stalked off.

"Okay," Althea said as she watched him go. "I kind of get the chaining thing now. What was that about?"

He knew but telling her would only make it worse. "Cadeyrn reminds me to remember my duty." He raised her hand to his lips. "Dinnae fret. He'll have no reason."

Brennus sent Kelturan and the cooks to bring the morning meal, and sacks of food for the patrols and sentries to take with them. Bottles of *uisge beatha* began to appear, and the men toasted him and Althea with the whiskey as if they'd already taken vows. Although it was no time for celebrations, he let the men enjoy their drink while he sent Taran after the War Master.

"They're no' married yet, you fools," Kelturan snapped as he thumped the platters on the table and snatched a *uisge beatha* bottle from a laughing clansman. He brought a bowl of Althea's odd oat mash to her and handed the bottle to Brennus. "I dinnae ken if 'tis a wise match for you, Chieftain. The lady eats like a pregnant sow and has a tongue like a boar's tusk."

Althea scowled at him. "Did you just call me two kinds of pig?"

"I cannae keep her out of the kitchens, so should you change your mind, I'll have her." The cook surreptitiously dropped some raspberries in her bowl. "Should you no', a sound beating every day should sweeten her temper."

"I know every single poisonous plant that grows around here," she told Kelturan. "And you never pay attention to what's in your mug. That could be tragic."

"Mayhap two beatings." The cook trudged off.

Brennus stole one of her berries. "'Twould seem you've made another conquest, my lady."

"Kelturan is not allowed to take a wife," she told him flatly. "Ever."

After they shared the morning meal with

the clan and Althea changed out of the dress for the journey, Brennus left Ruadri in charge of the stronghold. The chieftain took Althea with him to meet Cadeyrn and Taran down by the water. Cadeyrn brought a small keg to her and opened the top. Instead of containing whiskey, the inside was lined with leather.

"For your dress, my lady," the War Master said.

"Ah," she said and carefully tucked it inside.

As Cadeyrn sealed the keg, she moved against Brennus' side. Touching her made him wish they could delay the journey another week. "Once under the water you're to hold onto me. I'll be your breath, my lady."

Althea looked dubious as she nodded, and then she gave him a sharp look. "I dreamed about you kissing me underwater before I woke up here. You brought me to Dun Mor this way."

"You've found me out." He skimmed her lower lip with his thumb. "'Twas in truth our first kiss."

"If we're to meet the McAra by mid-day," Cadeyrn called to them, "we must go now."

Brennus needed his War Master with him to negotiate with the horse-breeders, but when they returned to Dun Mor he'd have to put to rest his growing hostility.

"He's upset about something else, not you," Althea said quietly. "He's been asking me a lot of questions about the other women who were taken. I don't know why, but I think he's really worried about them."

Like Ruadri was about the black-haired healer, Brennus thought as he took Althea's hand and led her into the currents.

Holding her as he bonded with the water reminded him, too, of the night they'd met. He greatly preferred her awake and nervous to limp and bloody, especially when his transformation made her eyes widen and her lips part.

"You turn into water," she whispered, touching her fingers to his face.

"Dinnae freeze me," Brennus said and covered her mouth with his as he thought of the loch nearest the McAra stronghold. Breathing with her as light and froth swirled around them, he let himself merge with the water itself. He could feel his clansmen beside him as they streamed through the highlands and down into the valleys to the northwest. He swallowed Althea's gasp as he surfaced with her in the loch and swam with her to the shallows.

"That was just like going on the biggest, longest water slide in the world," she said, laughing like a girl as she waded out of the water beside him. Cadeyrn lugged their journey packs out of the loch, while Althea took the keg a discrete distance into the adjoining woodland and changed.

When she emerged into the dancing light reflected from the loch, Brennus caught his breath. The fiery copper of her braided hair shone above star-bright eyes, their lochan-blue lit from within. The gown, though dazzling its finery, seemed scant next to the beauty of her face. As she neared and her delicate lips gently curved upward, his chest swelled in knowing that her smile was for him. He offered her his hand and beamed down at her when she took it.

"No' in my time or in this time," he said, enveloping her hand in both of his, "or any of the centuries between has so lovely a lady graced a chieftain's arm."

She'd been about to make a reply when Taran cleared his throat. Brennus thought to melt the man with a glare but went still when he saw a bulging fist holding a dagger to his Horse Master's throat.

"Stand your ground, lads," a low, grating voice said.

Chapter Twenty

✦✦✦

LTHEA LOOKED UP to see dozens of men with swords and large, spike-headed hammers emerging from behind the trees and marching down toward the loch.

Brennus pushed her behind him. "We're no' intruders. I've come to buy horses from your clan. The McAra laird expects us." He nodded at Taran. "My clansman came before, to bargain with him."

"So, you're a clan," the oldest of the warriors said. "Why do you no' wear the same tartan?" He jerked his chin at the war master. "I ken that as Gordon, but you wear the MacFarlan."

Althea muffled a groan. The clothing

the druids had given the Skaraven had included new wool tartans for every man, but in varied patterns. Ruadri mentioned to her that they had been contributed by several clans allied with the druids. Since the Skaraven had never been permitted to wear tartans during their former lives, they didn't understand the significance of the designs.

"Tell him that they're gifts from friends," she murmured quickly to Brennus. "And don't attack them. I think they're just being cautious."

"Our allies gave us the tartans," he said, growling the words. "If your laird doesnae want our gold, we'll leave."

"The laird awaits you in the glen," the clansman told him. "He'll decide when you go." He made a beckoning gesture with his sword.

Cadeyrn came to stand beside them. "Too many to fight and protect our lady here. They've likely brought mounts."

"Watch her back." Putting his arm around her, Brennus guided her up from the rocks and through the trees to enter the clearing beyond.

The McAra men closed around them, shoving Taran to join them.

"No horses," he muttered to Brennus.

Althea didn't understand why they were worried about horses when men with swords surrounded them. As they were marched through the tall grass she thought of her freezing power, and then remembered what had happened to Brennus's shackles last night when she'd lost her temper. She couldn't imagine using it on another human being, but to defend herself she might have to.

In the center of the glen sat a flat-topped rock, on which lay a short, slender man dressed in a dark blue jacket, black trousers and well-fitted dark leather boots. He looked as if he were sleeping, but as they approached he sat up and dusted off his sleeves, which ended in snowy lace cuffs.

The oldest clansman approached the man, bowed, and said, "Four intruders, my lord. They claim you invited them."

The man hopped off the rock, adjusted the hem of his jacket, and walked in front of them as if inspecting new troops.

When she saw his face, Althea felt stunned.

With his blue-black hair, crystalline eyes and white skin the man looked so much like Emeline they might have been siblings.

"I remember you," he said to Taran. "You claimed to be Clan Skaraven. I am Laird Maddock McAra." His gaze passed over Cadeyrn and Brennus before it locked on Althea. "Gods blind me, but you're a beauty."

"My thanks, sir," Althea said, trying to sound as Scottish as possible. "We've come as you asked."

"Hmmmm." Maddock glanced at his clansman. "If you must end them, dinnae slit that lovely throat. She'd make a fine bedding wench."

Brennus made an ugly sound.

"And you would be Chieftain, and the lady's husband." The laird gave him a lazy smile. "You've a formidable name. The McAra owe our bloodline to Brennus of the Skaraven. Mayhap to honor him I shall no' have you killed."

"The McAra owe more than their bloodline to us," Brennus said suddenly. "'Tis a debt that remains unsettled between our clans, written on a scroll that your tribe swore to preserve until we returned to collect."

Maddock laughed. "You ken the legend. How engaging. Do you claim right to it?"

"I do," Brennus said.

McAra snapped his fingers, and one of the men rushed over and held out a short tube made of stone. The laird took it in his languid grip, opening one end and shaking out an ancient scroll. "We McAra didnae forget Brennus or the debt. For hundreds of generations we've kept our word. Every laird since our tribe became a clan have sworn to preserve the scroll and repay the debt by any means desired by the Skaraven. Tell me what Brennus wrote on the scroll, Chieftain, and you shall have whatever you wish from my clan."

The McAra clansmen all drew their swords and moved in closer to the Skaraven.

"Only if you cannae tell me what the scroll contains," the laird warned him, "my men shall kill all of you, here and now."

Althea jumped as Brennus reached out and snatched the ancient parchment from Maddock's hands. Before anyone could speak he crushed it between his palms and flung the crumbled bits and dust into the wind.

The laird's face mottled with bright red patches as he drew his sword. "For that, you slee fack, I'll cut off your head. Slowly."

"You dinnae need the scroll anymore, McAra." Brennus bent down and used his finger to draw the shape of a large horse in the dirt, and then added a raven on its side. "'Tis what I drew on it when I gave it to Ara, the Pritani headman who made the vow. My clan and I saved him and his tribe from being slaughtered by the Viking."

Maddock stared at the drawing in the soil. "None but the living McAra laird ever knew what the scroll contained. You've come from the dead to collect the debt."

"I've come to buy horses," the chieftain told him. "I want naught else but friendship with your clan."

The laird shouted for his men to leave them. Once the clansmen were out of earshot he asked, "The druids kept their vow? They awakened you as immortals?" When Brennus reluctantly nodded the sword dropped from the McAra's hand, and then he knelt down and bowed his head.

"'Tis my honor, and that of my clan, to serve you, Chieftain. You shall have our finest horses, and a feast tonight to welcome your return to our realm. We shall from this day hence be your most loyal mortal allies and keep your secrets. This I pledge on my life and the lives of my clan." He sighed. "May this repay our debt to you?"

Brennus helped Maddock to his feet and clasped his forearm. "Aye, and more."

While the laird walked off to speak to his men, Althea blew out a long breath. "That turned out better than I thought. Was he serious about the feast, though?"

"'Tis an old midland custom, to offer food and rooms for the night to favored guests," Taran said, nodding. "'Twould no' be wise to refuse. Ruadri warned me they might take offense if I didnae stay for a meal when I came before. I cannae think what they may do if you dinnae attend a feast in our honor."

"I am dressed for a party," she said as she looked down at her gown, and then saw how Brennus was scowling. "Mortal allies are probably as valuable as horses. I think we should stay for it, as long as they agree we can leave in the morning."

The chieftain nodded and said as much to Maddock when he returned. The laird beamed and let out a sharp whistle. From the other side of the glen what looked like a hundred men rode out of the trees and galloped toward them. The horses they rode were large, muscular mounts with hides in every shade of brown. Taran smiled as he watched the riders come to sudden stops and form ranks that were ten across and ten deep.

"I reckon these should please you," the laird told Brennus as they walked over to inspect the mounts. "They're battle-trained, so they'll no' turn and run from your enemies. Saddled or bare-backed they'll carry you for ten leagues without rest."

Brennus checked the first mount's teeth and ran his hand along the horse's strong neck. "How are they in water?"

"Fearless. We begin taking them through rivers and into the loch as yearlings," Maddock said proudly. "Come and let me show you this mare for your lady wife."

As Brennus and Maddock went to look at the mare, Althea saw Taran already walking down the ranks, touching a nose or a shoulder here and there. The horses in turn watched him with visible interest, some even turning their heads to look at him.

"'Twill be good to have a herd for Tran to look after again," Cadeyrn said to her. "He's more horse than warrior."

"So, I guess you won't gut the chieftain?" When he started to walk away from her she got in front of him. "Hey, that crap you pulled this morning was nasty, even for you. But you were looking at me, not Brennus. So, here's your chance to hash it out with me. Just what is your problem?"

He looked up at the sky, and then shook his head. "You dinnae ken what we were. What 'twas like for us. They trained us to fear naught. To hold back naught. 'Tis still with us, inside us. The Skaraven dinnae retreat from a battle of any kind."

Apparently, it had nothing to do with her after all. "You think Brennus is wrong about the clan living as free men."

"We ken naught but battle. 'Twas why we

were bred and trained. 'Tis all we shall ever ken." He dragged a hand over his face. "'Tis no' my place to meddle. Only think on it, my lady, and mayhap you shall see as I do." He strode off.

For the rest of the day Althea kept replaying that odd conversation in her head. Even when they were ushered into the McAra's enormous castle, with all its splendid tapestries and furnishings, she kept watching the War Master. What had he been trying to tell her? She tried to reason it away. Cadeyrn was in charge of all things war and battle, so he probably thought of nothing else. None of the Skaraven ever said anything straight out. Still, she had the feeling that she'd missed something important.

Once they'd been introduced to the laird's wife and children, Althea and Brennus were escorted to the solar to rest. Maids brought in bread and cheese for them, along with some very strong, pulpy wine before hurrying out. But despite the hospitable spread, Brennus wore his unsettled face.

"I know you don't want to trust outsiders," Althea said as soon as they were alone. "But the laird just made good on a twelve-hundred-year-old IOU, and he swore to keep your secrets."

"'Tis no' the laird that troubles me. He kens that the druids meant to awaken us as immortals, as if some part of his clan's legend. No, 'tis no' that. McAra told me a dire storm from the west is coming. There'll be no time to take the horses back to Dun Mor. I have summoned the clan to us." He took hold of her hands. "'Tis more at work here than I fathom."

She rested her head against his shoulder. "We'll figure it out."

Cadeyrn came in to report on Taran, who had returned to Dun Mor to gather the clan and what weapons they needed for the rescue mission. The War Master had also gotten a look at the castle's layout, household guards, and the clan's patrols. He'd also found a spot near the kitchens where they could easily slip out after the feast and return home.

"Why?" Althea asked. "We're not taking the horses back, and the clan is coming to us at dawn."

"You shall be safer at Dun Mor, my lady," Cadeyrn said.

"'Twill no' be necessary," Brennus said and set down his wine. "Althea stays." He fixed the War Master with a glare. "You may go, Cade, if you've no stomach for your duty."

For a minute she thought the War Master might lunge at her lover, something she knew would end up trashing the solar and both of them.

"Why don't we all stay?" she said gayly, stepping between them. It was a move that redefined being between the rock and the hard place, but it seemed to dispel the impending disaster. "I'd feel better if Cadeyrn was here to keep an eye on my back." She looked from one man to the other. "I mean, the McAra never swore an oath to be my ally, right? I could still end up a bedding wench."

Brennus gave his War Master a direct look. "No' on my life, my lady."

"Nor mine. I shall stand watch." Cadeyrn walked out into the hall and let the door slam behind him.

Chapter Twenty-One

᪥

AT DAWN AFTER a long night's ride across the highlands, Hendry reined in his horse and gazed down at the druid settlement. Mounds of earth erupted on either side of him as the *caraidean* rose from their tunnels. They shook off the dirt clinging to their body wards as they gathered around him. Aon came forward, and breathed in the air.

"'Tis the stench of the Dawn Fire," he said.

As always, mortals could be depended on to betray their betters, Hendry thought as he dismounted and tethered his horse. "My friends, this day we take justice for what was visited upon us. We punish those who sought

in vain to thwart us. At long last, we triumph."
He gestured at the settlement. "Kill everything
that moves, but bring Flen to me alive."

Aon barreled toward the druid's cottages,
and the giants hurtled down the slopes after
him. Hendry moved to a higher spot in order
to watch. Maintaining a distance during the
first wave of slaughtering allowed him to keep
his robes clean, and he took great pleasure in
seeing the *caraidean* at their work. Later, he
would describe every moment to Murdina
while he pleasured her. His recounts always
made her climax until she wept.

Minutes passed, and while the giants
smashed their way into the cottages, none
emerged with helpless, writhing victims to tear
asunder. Hendry strode down to the center of
the settlement, where by now there should
have been a pile of druid carcasses. Not a
single body had been brought out for him to
admire. Aon came to him, his eyes glittering
with unreleased rage as he hurled an empty
cooking pot into the dead ashes of the ritual
pit fire.

"Gone."

"All?" When he nodded Hendry cast a

seeking spell, which returned to him with nothing. "It cannae be. The mortal swore that he delivered doves to them no' threeday past." This new betrayal made him clench his fists. "We shouldnae have killed him so quickly."

"Cold hearths, empty rooms, larders empty. The Dawn Fire have fled." The giant shouted for Dha, who stumbled over to them. "Tell the others to smash their things. Leave naught sound." To Hendry he said, "Flen heard we ended his old friend. He didnae trust in his silence."

"How sad he shall be when I tell him that Gwyn Embry bit through his tongue in order to hold it." He looked around them, furious that his wily old enemy had eluded them again. "Aon, we must find them. We cannae begin to remake the world as long as the Dawn Fire breathe. As long as that old bastart might interfere."

The giant shrugged. "Use the female."

"I cannae risk her." A throbbing set in at his temple, as always when he thought of her. "She must remain protected."

"Aon." Tri jittered in front of him, his

damaged face filled with confusion. "No druid or beast. Naught to kill. What do now?"

"Find pretty," Aon said. "Make ugly." Once Tri scurried off the giant glanced at Hendry. "You dinnae like Tri."

"'Tis no' a matter of liking but needing. We shouldnae bring him with us," Hendry said, as kindly as he could. "He becomes muddled and distressed."

"Tri doesnae much understand human words. They split his mind when they put him in the henge." He watched the other giant rooting through a flower bed. "Still he remains loyal to me. Like your lady, Wood Dream."

"Aye." The reminder made Hendry's anger roil higher. He could not return to the encampment with nothing to show for their journey. Murdina would be livid. Nor could he go without feeding his own rage fire a sacrifice. "Show me Flen's hovel, please. I want to search it."

"Aon," Tri called to him, sounding excited. "Come see pretty. Come see make ugly."

Coig kicked over a pear tree in front of the house Aon identified as Flen's, and prepared to ram it through the front entry.

"No' this one," Aon said. "Go help Tri."

"Aye, please." Hendry glanced over at the damaged giant, who had dragged a basin out into the sunlight. Orange light fountained up at once, spilling over itself back into the basin. "And take that away from him. 'Tis a torch fount."

Just as the words left his lips Tri thrust his hand into the light, which changed to flame on contact and raced up his arm. Shrieking, the now-flaming giant ran around waving his arms and showering the cottages with fiery embers. Thatching caught light and began to burn. Coig hefted the pear tree under his arm and trudged after him.

"By the gods, so he can be useful." Hendry picked up a bruised pear and entered the cottage.

Inside the air reeked of calming herbs and benevolent spells. The old druid had lived there so long he'd tainted every object and furnishing with his personal stink. Hendry breathed it in deeply, feeding that much of Flen to the grinding, tireless furnace in his chest. When he checked the spell chamber he found only bare shelves where there should have been a treasure-trove of crystals and talismans. The cabinets, trunks and baskets in the adjoining bed chamber stood open and empty.

Aon ducked his head to look in at him. "'Tis a message left for you in the cooking room."

Sweat beaded on his brow as he came out of the room. Hendry had been careful to ward the encampment and the *caraidean* against far-seeing, convinced that would blind any attempt to find them or learn of their move-ments. Had Bhaltair somehow guessed they would be coming for him, even before the mortal told them of the settlement? Had he set a spell trap to imprison them for all eter-nity here?

In the kitchen, flour had been spilled all over the table, providing the canvas for the message. It had been written in a script so ancient only he or one of the giants could have deciphered it.

Too late.

Hendry's hands balled into fists and his jaw tightened.

A heavy hand clamped on his shoulder before Aon left.

The druid stood beside the table, unable to look away from the taunt Flen had left behind for him. Pride, the one weakness the old meddler had never overcome, must have spurred him to write it. To gloat from a safe distance over the triumph he now anticipated.

Through clenched teeth Hendry said, "I am no' yet defeated, old man."

With quaking hands, he scraped and shoved the flour into a rough mound. Though he'd been imprisoned without his focal stones or crystals, his spellwork was the match of none. Shutting his eyes tight he summoned the most powerful of viewing spells. He muttered the words, over and over, his voice growing louder with each incantation. Though the veins in his temples throbbed and his heart pounded in his ears, he said it again, and then again. Slowly he opened his eyes to a swirling ball of crimson sparkles that hovered over the table. With a mighty breath, he blew the flour into it.

Though some of the flour hissed and popped out of existence, enough remained swirling in the viewing ball. As Hendry watched, two indistinct forms coalesced. The short one he didn't know, but the other he knew too well.

"*Flen*," he muttered.

"Master," said the short one. Hendry bent forward to hear the dim voice. "Should we no' be making haste?"

Hendry watched as the old druid spread the flour on the table.

"The Skaraven serve us again," he assured her in his aged voice. "We've some time yet."

"But—"

"Calm yourself, child," he said, regarding her. "Soon our allies 'twill go to them by water. With the aid of the druidess who possesses the touch of ice, victory 'twill be ours." He stood back to survey the table and put a gnarled finger to his chin. Then he crooked up a corner of his mouth. "I have it."

As he reached to the flour, the vision suddenly ended and the globe of sparkles winked out. The flour it had suspended drifted back to the table in long tendrils as Hendry stumbled back and sat down hard on a stool. Breathing deeply, he put a hand to his chest.

"Gods," he gasped. "The conclave has gone mad."

To be brought back to life he knew the warrior-slaves would have been made immortals. Such a precious gift would render them almost impossible to kill. In the first century the clan had been menacing. Now as enemies they would rival the giants—no doubt exactly what Flen had intended. He had personally overseen the training of the Skaraven, and likely had tamed them with obedience spells and controlling wards as soon as he woke them from their graves.

That the warrior and the escaped female had disappeared into the lochan now made more sense. Flen must have used the Dawn Fire's magic to give the clan the ability to somehow use rivers and lochs as portals. Such would permit them to move in water as the giants did through the earth.

Hendry felt a plop of wetness fall on his hand and looked down to watch another join it. He touched the streaks on his face, and thought of Murdina pacing in the farmhouse, awaiting his return with Flen. He'd promised her that the old fool would die by her hand.

He'd hoped that a long and satisfying blood-letting would help restore her to sanity.

Now Flen's escape might push her over into the abyss.

But at least his vision spell had salvaged a sliver of hope. He glanced at the table and permitted himself a smirk. Yes, pride had been the old man's weakness. Some things didn't change.

The scent of burning pine made Hendry stand as flames erupted from beneath the old druid's table. It crawled through the flour, blackening it and the hateful message. He swept his hand to one side, and the table fell over to let loose the fire on the worn floor planks.

The Gods had not released them to return to their deaths, Hendry thought calmly as he left the burning kitchen. He took a bite of the browned pear and savored the taste of its overripe flesh. Such a pity the giants did not eat. When he took Flen from whatever hole he had crawled into, he might have fed him to them, one chunk of flesh at a time.

Hendry emerged from the cottage to see the rest of the settlement now merrily burning.

Aon stood with the other giants on its outskirts. They watched as Coig used an axe to chop the pear tree into a new form for Tri. Beside it his blackened remains streamed white smoke into the air.

No more shall we suffer. No more shall we submit. 'Tis time for the reckoning.

Hendry closed his eyes as his power burst out of him, and Flen's cottage exploded, hurling burning debris in all directions.

Chapter Twenty-Two

A T SUNSET THE McAra came to the solar to personally escort Althea and Brennus to the feast. As they walked with him through the corridors the laird apologized for not being better prepared.

"'Twould have been a grander celebration, Chieftain, if my servants had some months to prepare," he told Brennus. "My poulterers keep an adequate stock of squab and game birds, of course, and the hunters supply enough deer, hare and boar to feed the king's court. Still, I should have liked to offer a more impressive meal." He frowned. "Mayhap I should have ordered an ox slaughtered. Or do you crave a particular delicacy, my lady? Our ladies greatly favor milk-boiled eel."

Althea swallowed and smiled. "Ah, no, my lord."

Hundreds of McAra clansman and their wives packed the laird's great hall. The crowd fell silent as they bowed and curtseyed when Maddock entered. Althea admired their fine garments but felt more awed by the feast itself. Towering platters of meats and breads and enormous crocks of soups and stews crammed every table in sight. The dishes had been grouped by color, creating a rainbow effect across the hall. Serving maids stood ready with steaming ewers of sauces and bottles of dark wine. Behind them a trio of men filled tankards and goblets with whiskey from kegs the size of a compact car.

"Welcome, my kin," Maddock said, and clapped Brennus on the shoulder. "I present to you Chieftain Brennus of the Clan Skaraven, protectors of the McAra. He asks naught from us but friendship. So to honor our debt to his clan, we shall give him our loyalty. From this day forth, the McAra serve the Skaraven as sworn allies. Make your vow before him now."

"Tha mi a 'gealltainn," the men and women of the clan called out.

When Althea turned a quizzical look to Brennus, he leaned toward her. "I promise," he translated.

Guards marched through the assembly to open a long series of panels at the back of the hall, which revealed an outdoor courtyard lit by huge torches and furnished with long trestle tables. Musicians played lilting songs on lutes and reed pipes as the clan helped themselves to the food and went out to sit under the stars.

Althea and Brennus sat at the laird's table, along with Cadeyrn and Taran and the McAra's chieftains, stablemasters and garrison captains. Since her fake Scottish accent needed more practice Althea stayed quiet and listened to the men discuss the recent attacks on towns and villages to the west of their territory.

"I had word today of a druid settlement being burned in the northern highlands," Maddock told Brennus. "'Twas an odd thing, for they found no dead. Only great furrows in the ground. The same as found at the villages attacked and massacred by strange warriors.

One lad who survived swore they came from the ground, like giant voles."

Brennus exchanged a look with Cadeyrn. "In the time of Ara the Skaraven battled such an enemy. Carved wooden giants called the *famhairean,* they were brought to life by druid bloodshed. They could dig through the earth faster than the swiftest mount. With one clout they could crush the strongest warrior."

The men around the table fell silent as the laird nodded. "We, too, have legends of the *famhairean*, and the mad lovers who used them against mortal and druid kind. 'Twas said they met defeat in battle with your clan."

"For a time, aye, they did. The druids entrapped them for eternity in a spell prison." Brennus glanced at Althea. "They escaped and returned to seek vengeance against the Skaraven and the tree-knowers. They mean to rid the world of mortal kind."

Maddock took a long swallow from his tankard. "Do the Skaraven stand against them once more, Chieftain?"

"Aye. We shall fight the *famhairean* until we rid the world of them." Brennus grinned broadly. "And at dawn we shall ride into battle from here on our fine McAra horses."

The laird's men roared their approval and thumped the table with their fists so hard their trenchers jumped.

The laird stood and raised his whiskey. "May the Gods bless our clans with victory."

"Victory," his men said, and raised their drinks before draining them in one swallow.

The clan's pipers stood and played a loud, fierce tune. From the great hall two men dressed in stuffed, shaped burlap horse-and-rider costumes trotted out. Althea joined in with the general laughter as the two mock riders drew wooden swords and jousted at each other. After them came a group of young boys dressed in what had to be their fathers' tunics and tartans, in which they capered comically with the mock horsemen as they tried to steal their blades.

One of the boys brought a fistful of wildflowers to Althea, and bowed like a courtier as he presented them.

"My thanks," she told the lad, who blushed and hurried away to fling himself into the arms of the laird's wife. "How sweet."

"My youngest lad," Maddock said, sounding gloomy. "He'll no' take up the blade. Spends every day in the gardens troweling in the dirt and plucking posies." His mouth twitched. "Just as I did as a lad."

Althea felt Brennus stiffen beside her, and followed the direction of his gaze to the last performer entering from the hall. Two men wore a costume of white wool that had been stuffed and tied to resemble a giant stag, complete with a spiky rack of real, bleached horns. Instead of trotting through the tables, the mock-stag delicately minced its way toward the laird's table.

Brennus got to his feet as the stag stopped beside him, and stared down at the knots of wool that formed the eyes.

The stag bowed its straw and wool head to the chieftain before it walked into the shadows.

"The white stag was the symbol of our ancient Pritani tribe," Maddock said to Brennus. "'Twas no' meant to offend you, Chieftain."

"It doesnae," he said, and sat back down. Under the table he took hold of Althea's hand. "But I feel the hand of the Gods tonight, Maddock McAra."

The laird smiled. "Now you walk in my boots, Brennus Skaraven."

Once they had finished eating, Brennus formally thanked the laird and his lady for the generous feast, and took Althea upstairs to the rooms that had been provided for them and their men.

Althea smiled at the big cabinet bed draped in lace and festooned with flowers, and turned to see Brennus leaning against the door and watching her.

"It's been a long day," she said. "You must be tired."

He shook his head.

"The clan will be here at dawn," she said. Feeling a twinge of mischief, she moved to stand in the shaft of moonlight streaming in from the high, narrow window covered with a fine netting. "We should get some sleep."

The chieftain turned and inspected the door, which had no lock or bolt bar. He dragged one of the dainty chairs by the fireplace over to it, tipped it, and wedged it under the knob.

Althea reached behind her waist for the ties that cinched the back of her gown, tugging them loose. "I think I'd better stay in this. Unless you want to get a maid to help me undress."

Brennus shook his head again as he advanced on her.

She turned her back on him as she went over to look through the window netting. "Oh, what a nice view. I want to sleep on this side of the bed."

His hands gripped her waist. "'Tis sleep you want, my lady?"

Althea loved that he didn't hesitate to touch her anymore. "I don't know." She bent over, resting her elbows on the sill and tilting her hips, just enough to brush the back of her skirts against the front of his trousers. "We've seen the horses, met everyone, and even had dinner and a show. Maybe the laird has some board games in here."

"Are you bored, my lady?" Brennus murmured as he slid one hand around to hold her just under her breasts, and used the other to tug loose the ties over her spine.

"One thing I'm never with you, Bren, is

bored." She closed her eyes as he pressed his mouth to her nape.

Her bodice began to sag, and his big hand tugged it away from her bare breasts.

"You didnae wear that hooked band today," Brennus said, stroking his fingers over her curves.

"The straps would have shown, and I'm not sure how to explain what a bra is to medieval people." She caught her breath as he tugged on one tight nipple. "Don't you believe me?"

"No," he murmured against her ear. "I suspect you like being bare under your gown. To feel the silk on your skin. To be ready for my touch."

She rubbed her bottom slowly over the straining bulge of his erection. "Maybe I wanted you to think about it too. You knew I was naked under this gown."

"Every moment of this day." He cupped her breasts and kneaded them slowly. "I want you naked for me now, Althea."

Shivering, she straightened, and pulled her arms out of the gown. Leaning back against him, she wriggled until she eased the bodice over her hips, and let it and the skirts fall to the floor.

"Bathe in the moonlight for me." Brennus took her hands, bracing them on either side of the window, and nudged her feet apart. "Your skin glows in it."

She heard him undressing behind her, and lifted her face into the soft white light, hoping that it made her look as beautiful as he made her feel.

His heat moved over her as he came closer, and then his hands gripped her hips as he shifted her over him. The slick head of his cock found the wet, swollen seam of her sex, and slid against it to part her folds and graze her pulsing clit. She tried to impale herself on him, but he eluded her, and continued the slow, sliding strokes against her pussy.

"'Tis turnabout, my lady," Brennus said, dropping a kiss on her shoulder. "You had your way with me at Dun Mor. Now I'll have mine."

His way was to drive her to climax with his torturous rubbing shaft, she thought, and dragged in a steadying breath. "Maybe you should chain me."

"I think on it." He pulled her hair away from her neck and tasted her skin there. "No' with chains, but silk laces." He barely moved against her now, the ridge of his cockhead working back and forth over her clit. "I think on having you kneel before me, your pretty mouth open for me." He nuzzled her ear. "Some night would you take me thus, Althea? As I watch you do it?"

"Only if you don't tie my hands." She felt the need like fever now. It was going to burn her alive. "I want them on you too."

Brennus reached between their sexes to work his satiny bulb into the clenching ellipse of her softness. Once he had pushed in until she enveloped his cockhead, he clamped an arm around her waist and skewered her with his shaft.

"When McAra spoke of making you his bedding wench, I near snapped his neck," he said, his voice taking on a dark edge. "No man facks you but me, Althea."

His jealousy scared her a little, but it also gave her a fierce satisfaction. "Same here. No bedding wenches for you—" She lost the rest of it in a cry of delight as he stroked in and out of her. "Oh, Brennus. Oh, finally."

"Aye, I ken how you crave this." He drove into her deeper, slowing his thrusts as she tightened around him. "As do I."

Her breasts bounced from the force of his pumping, relentless cock, and Althea cried out as the drenching, throbbing core of her need billowed around him. He must have felt it, for he lifted her off her feet and worked her on his shaft, driving her sex over him as he plowed deep.

Althea whimpered, trying not to scream, but he sensed that too. His hand clamped over her mouth as he told her, "Squeeze me again with your quim. Bite my flesh. Do as I tell you, Althea."

She drove her teeth into his hand and gripped his cock, and her body stiffened as her climax ripped through her. She heard him mutter low, rough words against her ear as he fucked her through the explosions of sensation. Then, somehow, she was falling, and Brennus was on top of her on the bed, still pumping between her thighs, still pounding her spasming pussy. The cabinet around them began to rock and squeak, but Althea couldn't stop him. She writhed under him, pinned between his hard body and her own needs, which flared up as if she'd never come. Then it came again, bliss atop bliss, and she flung her arms around his neck as she brought his panting mouth down to hers.

His muscles bunched and stretched under her touch once, twice, and then he shook all over as he pulsed inside her. The jets of his seed bathed her from within, soft and warm and wet, and when he collapsed on her she held him as tightly as she could.

"No, don't do that," she whispered when he shifted as if he meant to roll away. "I want you right here."

Brennus lifted his head to kiss her brow, sighing against it before he looked into her eyes. "You would kill that little laird in bed."

"That's your fault. You've reset my standards to impossible." She didn't want to move again, but dawn wasn't that far away. That thought also reminded her of the conversation they needed to have about the future, their future, but this wasn't the right time for that, either. "But we can't sleep like this. It'll be a

replay of last night, when I had my way with
you three, no, four times."

Gently he withdrew from her, and tugged
back the coverlet to drape it over their hot,
damp bodies. As he gathered her against his
side, he said, "'Twill be well, Althea. I promise
you."

"I know." She closed her eyes and rubbed
her cheek over his ink, drifting off a moment
later.

The sound of footsteps dragged her
awake, and she sat up to see Brennus still
sleeping beside her. He'd kicked off the coverlet, and stretched out, taking up most of
the bed.

Even immortal medieval warriors were
bed hogs, she thought, and smothered a yawn.
That was when she spotted two shadows
moving through the light coming under the
door from the hall.

Wrapping the coverlet around her, she
went to the door and removed the chair in
order to peek out. In the passage Cadeyrn was
walking down the length of the hall, only to
turn and walk back toward her.

Althea slipped out of the chamber and

gently closed the door before she regarded him. "What are you doing out here?"

"My duty," he said drily. "I dinnae fall asleep if I walk, my lady. Go back to bed. 'Twill soon be dawn."

"Brennus didn't order you to stand guard. We're fine. Go to bed yourself." When he shook his head she beckoned to him and moved to the end of the hall. "Brennus wanted to kill the laird for just talking about bedding me. If anyone comes in our room who isn't Skaraven, they're going to die. Badly. You don't have to do this." From his stony expression he didn't agree. "I've got this all wrong. Okay, *why* are you standing guard?"

"'Twas my turn." He looked up at the ceiling. "Taran, Ruadri and I stand guard each night outside the chieftain's chamber. Some others as well." He met her gaze. "'Tis to protect you, my lady. To be ready should you call out or scream."

"But Brennus is right there and he would…oh, no." She took a step back from him. "You haven't just been standing guard. You've been *eavesdropping*."

"'Twas plain to us that you and the chieftain…" He stopped and then tried again. "We didnae listen at the door. We've only been ready to break in and pull him away if need be."

"You thought he was going to hurt me." Her eyes widened. "In bed."

Cadeyrn looked as uncomfortable as she felt now. "The chieftain told you about the pleasure lasses brought to us. 'Tis all we ken of females. We worried he wouldnae…be proper and gentle with you."

"Well, he is. And when he's not, I like that too. Forget I said that." She rubbed her forehead and dropped her arm. "Cade, I know you have good intentions, and I'm the first woman you've ever talked to, but you're wrong. Brennus would cut off his own arm before he hurt me. Also, what he and I do in private is *really* none of your business." A thought occurred to her. "This is why you were so angry with him this morning. Why you tried to warn me later."

He nodded slowly. "'Twas meant kindly, my lady." He glanced at the chamber door. "Do you still wish to return to the future?"

"For what? He's here. I love him." Until

this moment she hadn't consciously decided that, or realized how deeply she felt about Brennus. "I'm not going anywhere."

Cadeyrn stunned her by enveloping her in his arms and giving her a hard hug. Immediately he stepped back. "I'll find my bed now."

Althea watched him walk down and disappear into another chamber. "Mercy, does this mean I have to have a talk with the entire clan?"

Chapter Twenty-Three

❧

A T DAWN THE Skaraven arrived
en masse at the McAra stronghold,
and assembled outside the huge
stables as their new mounts were brought out.
Taran thankfully remembered to bring Althea
a change of clothes from her carryall, but
once she'd dressed Brennus came in with a
stack of oddly-shaped iron plates.

"The storm will arrive within the hour."
He put the iron down on the bed and brought
the biggest piece over to her. "I had Kanyth
fashion these for you."

As he loosened some straps attached to the
sides and top of the plate she realized what it
was. "You had him make armor for me?"

"You arenae immortal, Althea. A single

blade thrust can end you." He tried to put it over her and scowled as she sidestepped him. "Come here."

"Stay there. Now, imagine a blade coming at me." She picked up a smaller piece of the armor. "I touch it." She froze the iron, and let it drop to the floor. It shattered like glass. "Any questions?"

Brennus tossed the chest plate onto the bed, and put on his chieftain glower. "I'll have you taken back to Dun Mor and held there until we return with them."

"Held there? You couldn't even keep me in the *eagalsloc*." She saw his frustration and went to him. "I know the map isn't accurate enough, but I'll remember the location of the barn when I'm there. Besides, the other women need to see a familiar face when we grab them, or they'll freak out. You know I'm not helpless, and I can protect myself. Also, I have the awesome freezing power, which may come in handy. I'm going with you."

Though the glower had left, he was clearly far from convinced. His brow furrowed, but he nodded.

"Then you go as my lady." He pulled the

leather lacing from the top of his tunic, and took off his clan ring, which he slid onto the lacing. "Mine to love, and to wed, as soon as we return to Dun Mor."

Once he tied it around her neck, she caressed the gleaming black ring. "So you *do* want me to stay in the fourteenth century."

"I want you with me." He tipped up her chin. "I must remain here with my brethren."

"Okay." His reaction made her grin. "I decided to stay last night, while I was talking to Cade out in the hall, and no, I'm not going to tell you about that. We have helpless women to rescue, Chieftain. Come on."

Once outside the castle Althea saw the approaching storm spreading like a dark cancer on the horizon. As the giants' encampment lay due west, they'd be in very rough weather when they emerged from the lochan.

"Chieftain, there's lightning in those clouds," she heard Kanyth say to Brennus, and looked over to see the Weapons Master's worried expression. "You'll recall how much it likes me. Mayhap I should go ahead of the clan."

The chieftain shook his head. "Ride at the

rear, Ka." He caught Althea's gaze. "Kanyth's power also draws lighting. 'Tis been striking him since boyhood."

"I didn't even know Kanyth *had* a power," she pointed out. "We have a lot to talk about when we get back."

"Oh, aye," he said, and gave her temple a kiss.

They walked over to the stables, where the clan greeted them with smiles and nods. They'd already gone into battle-silent mode, Althea decided, which wasn't a bad thing. A lot of chatter right now would be distracting.

"Fair morning, pretty lass," Althea said and patted the nose of the mare that the McAra had hand-picked for her. Brennus helped her up into the small saddle, which felt stiff and unyielding but fit her bottom well enough. "Are you sure you can handle taking me and two horses through the water by yourself?"

"I'll take your other arm, my lady," Cadeyrn said. "Just to be safe."

The McAra had come up with the solution to keeping the mounts from being spooked by the clan's water-traveling, and now came to

hand her the wide leather browband to attach
to her mare's bridle.

"Remember, my lady, fasten the band to
the center stud on the cheekpieces before you
enter the loch," Maddock told her. "'Twill
cover her eyes completely."

She glanced over at the other Skaraven,
who had tucked identical browbands in their
belts. "My thanks, my lord."

"Gods speed." He turned to Brennus. "If
the Skaraven dinnae return, Chieftain, the
McAra shall take up your cause."

Brennus clasped forearms with him. "Con-
sult the druids if you do. They've the power
you'll need."

Althea hadn't ridden a horse since she'd
sold her uncle's farm, but the familiar rocking
rhythm quickly came back to her. It also
helped that the mare had an almost liquid
gait, and legs long enough to keep up with
Brennus and Cadeyrn's bigger mounts.

They halted at the shore of the loch, with
the clan forming a single line behind them.
Althea fit the browband to her mare's bridle
and urged her into the shallows.

Brennus and Cadeyrn took hold of her as

they transformed and submerged with all three horses. Althea held her breath and hung onto the reins. The mare tensed under her as bubbling light rose around them.

Streaming through the water on a horse felt much scarier than in Brennus's arms, but a few seconds later the men surfaced and guided her and their horses out of the lochan.

Icy wind and needle-sharp rain pelted them as they rode out into the storm. Overhead white-hot veins streaked through the swollen clouds, followed by a rumbling boom of thunder.

Their mounts skittered until they removed the browbands, which helped calm the horses. One by one the clan came riding out of the water, shedding their transformations as they joined the chieftain.

Cadeyrn and Ruadri rode a few yards ahead, scanning the forest before they trotted back to Brennus.

"I sense no spell traps or wards," the shaman said as he wiped the rain from his face. "'Tis some magic deep within the woods, but 'twould be from the farm."

Cadeyrn pointed to the north side of the

forest. "The far trail offers more protection. We should ride and take cover at a vantage point to scout them."

The chieftain nodded, and signaled to the rest of the clan, who assembled into three long ranks. The archers among them also carried buckets attached to their saddles.

"What are those for?" Althea asked.

"A surprise for our wood friends," Brennus replied quickly before taking up position in front.

The other men drew their swords and held them ready as they guided their mounts with one hand.

Riding into the dark forest put Althea's nerves on edge, as if dozens of hidden eyes watched them. The frigid rain had also soaked through her clothes, chilling her to the bone. Yet she saw no sign of the giants, and hoped that they would hold onto the element of surprise. Now all she had to do was recognize the way.

Brennus shifted his horse in front of hers, and Ruadri came up to flank her with Cadeyrn. She turned her head to smile at the shaman, and saw one of the trees beside him sprout two eyes and a snarling mouth.

"Ru, watch out," she shouted.

She wheeled her mare about, cutting of the shaman as she reached for the giant with her hands. Though the air temperature dropped, the giant sidestepped her. She urged her mare forward.

"Althea, no!" she heard Brennus shout.

A hard blow from behind knocked her to the ground, where she was dragged by her leg into the brush. She screamed as she saw all the trees lining the trail attack Brennus and the clan, but a huge wooden hand slammed into her jaw, and she blacked out.

∞※∞

"MAYBE WE COULD NEGOTIATE WITH THEM," Rowan said as she peered out of the wooden slats. "I'll offer to babysit the really batshit one, and out of extreme gratitude they'll let us go back to the barn."

Emeline sighed. "Rowan, please."

"We're never going back to the bloody barn," Lily muttered.

Rowan silently agreed with her, not that she'd admit it out loud. No, she had to keep everyone's spirits up, because in a few days they were either going to die of exposure, starvation, dehydration, or all three. Since Hendry had started leaving on his three or four day trips away from the farm, they had to depend on the guards or Murdina for rations. Since the uglies hated them, and the druidess had gone almost completely cuckoo's nest, rations came very infrequently. At one point they'd had to eat snow for water.

Ochd sometimes brought them oatcakes, which he passed to Rowan when none of the other guards could see. He always said the same thing too: "Hide. Dinnae let Coig see."

She shared everything with the other women, but Perrin barely touched hers and Emeline's jaw was so sore she was having trouble chewing.

That was thanks to Coig, who had been the most inventive guard at Camp Seriously Crazy. Now and then, probably out of psycho boredom, he would come over to poke sticks in the cage to try to jab them. He was good at it. They all had big ugly bruises from his efforts. Lily had once grabbed the stick and jerked it out of his hand, but he'd just opened the cage, dragged her out and took it from her. Then he'd beaten her until the stick broke.

Coig also liked beating them—a lot. If Hendry left him behind and took the other, reasonably sane guards, by the third day he'd haul one of them out and chase them around, beating their legs, punching them in the face, or tossing them into something. If they didn't try to get away he'd beat them unconscious. Either way, once he'd had his fun he'd put them back and later claim to the druids that they'd try to escape.

For some reason he never took Rowan out of the cage. She'd even offered to take Perrin's place for one of his beatdowns, but Coig just ignored her.

Things had gone from bad to worse, but she knew they were never going to get better. If Rowan didn't figure a way to get back to the barn, she was pretty sure Coig was going to kill them while they were not trying to escape.

Emeline sat up and looked over at the trail. "Someone's coming."

ALTHEA CAME to as she was dragged across the muddy ground between the farmhouse and the barn. Ochd jerked her to her feet, and tied her arms behind a tall, burned oak trunk. She grimaced as the guard wrapped rough burlap around her hands before binding her wrists.

Wearing a sodden cloak and holding a gleaming scythe, Murdina walked up to her and held the curved blade under her nose. "Foolish wench. When we learned you'd betrayed us to those Skaraven bastarts, we removed the wards from the forest, and put them on the lochan."

She could see the biggest of the guards now, trudging through the mud toward a huge wooden cage. Inside were the four other women, huddled together and looking much more battered than they had when she'd escaped. Her heart ached to see how gaunt Perrin had grown, and the bruises on Lily and Emeline. Rowan appeared to be in the best shape, but she had a wild look in her eyes as she stared back at Althea.

"Bring them to me, Dha," Murdina called.

He opened one end of the cage and reached in. The women tried to avoid his hand by scattering to the back, but he tossed out Emeline and Perrin, and then locked in Rowan and Lily.

A hard slap made Althea stare at the crazy druidess, who a moment later caressed her throbbing cheek.

"Poor lass, you've had such an ordeal. Did those brutes rape you? Their masters never permitted them near any female unless they wore chains, or so Hendry said. I'll help you get revenge on them." She beckoned to Dha, who hauled Emeline and Perrin over to her, and shoved them to their knees. "I dinnae care for rain. Make it snow."

Althea peered at her. "What?"

"You have the touch of ice. 'Tis one of the greatest powers known to druid kind. In time you shall have only to think it, and freeze anything you wish." Murdina smiled gently. "You shall release it on the storm above us. All of it, just now, and make a blizzard so cold it shall freeze the Skaraven in their tracks. If you dinnae, Dha will crush these wench's skulls together, until their brains mix."

The guard seized Emeline and Perrin on either side of their faces, and pushed their heads together, making his huge hands into a vise.

☙❧

"No," Rowan shouted at Murdina as she jerked on the cage's wooden slats, trying to loosen them enough for her to get an arm out and dislodge the locking bar.

"Ro, stop," Lily said, trying to pull her back. "There's nothing you can do for her now."

"She's too weak. They'll kill her this time. Don't just sit there, help me."

When Lily shook her head Rowan launched herself at the slats, throwing her full weight into them. She bounced off and fell on her face. She shoved herself up and gripped the slats with her fingers. What was happening to Perrin? She couldn't see anything through this damn cage.

The slats slowly moved apart under her hands.

Rowan snatched her hands away, and then

reached between the slats, sliding her hand through easily. "What in God's name?"

She thought fast, recalling everything the crazy druids had said about them. The five of them were supposed to be druidesses, capable of great power blah blah blah. She'd heard them bickering when Hendry came back from burning a druid settlement, and he'd told Murdina that the flame-haired wench had the touch of ice, and could freeze solid whatever she touched. She hadn't thought of Althea having flame-colored hair because like the others she assumed she'd been killed trying to escape.

If Althea was able to freeze something by touching it…

Rowan put her hands on the slats again, and thought of making them twice as wide. This time they moved apart under her hands, creating a foot-wide gap.

"What are you doing?" Lily asked.

"Getting out of here." She looked over at Murdina and Dha, and then moved to the back of the cage. "Sit in the front so they don't see me. Do it, Stover."

As soon as Lily's body blocked hers Rowan

put her hands on the back of the cage and
thought of the slats separating to a gap wide
enough for her to crawl through. The cage
shook, and wood splintered, but when she let
go there was a Rowan-sized hole waiting
for her.

Without another word she crawled out,
running for the farmhouse, and the line of
clothes Murdina had hung out to dry and
never brought in. Taking down a snow-crusted
blanket, she wrapped herself in it and covered
her head.

The drifts around the farmhouse never
melted, and she stayed close to them as she
crept closer to where Dha had Perrin and
Emeline. She stopped at the woodpile long
enough to grab a big branch, which she
tucked under the blanket. When she looked
over again she could see Althea's white face,
and the red handprint blazing on her cheek.
Then she heard what Murdina ordered her to
do, and watched Dha trap Emeline and Perrin
between his hands.

Spear, she thought, and felt the wood
smooth and lengthen in her hand. When she
glanced inside the blanket she saw the branch

had changed into a smooth rod with a sharply pointed tip.

Rowan had become the darts champion at every watering hole she'd ever frequented. She just had to think of the spear like a really big dart.

She looked over at Althea, who spotted her in the same moment, but didn't give her away by turning her head. All the other woman did was make a tiny nod before she closed her eyes.

Dr. Useless thought she was going to kill *her*? Rowan felt like doing it just so she wouldn't be disappointed. The more she thought about it, however, the more it made sense. Kill the doc, no blizzard, and they'd be rescued by these Skaraven guys.

Only Dha would be pissed, and Perrin would die before the cavalry came. No, she had to stick to the original target.

Rowan moved to a spot where she had the best angle, and took out the spear. As Murdina moved closer to Althea, she hefted the giant-size dart and hurled it at the guard's face.

The spear buried itself in Dha's left eye, ramming through it into what Rowan hoped was his brain. He staggered backward, roaring with pain, and Perrin and Emeline fell into the mud.

"Great idea," Althea said as Rowan rushed past her. "Mind if I steal it?"

"Isn't that what you college nerds always do?" she snarled as she grabbed her sister, and helped her to her feet.

Without warning the temperature dropped from icy to Arctic.

A white shimmer moved through the rain, pulling the droplets together into long icicles. They grew larger as they came down, and then stopped short of impaling Murdina. Slowly they spun away from the druidess, collecting more rain as they grew thicker and longer. A bolt of lightning rammed down, striking a tree behind the farmhouse, and the flash of light made the icy spears glitter like some enormous, fragmented chandelier.

The crazy druidess turned around, looking at the floating ice as frost crept up her skirts and whitened cloak. She hurried up to Althea, who had frost-coated eyelashes and patches of ice sparkling on her face.

"Stop," she shrieked. "'Tis too much. Do you wish to die?"

Snowflakes drifted down from Althea's lips as they curved into a stiff smile. "To. Save. Him." She dragged in a choppy breath. "Yes."

Rowan held on grimly to her sister as she watched Althea's eyes go white and opaque as they froze. The ice spears almost dropped to the ground, but then they stopped, flew up and hurled themselves at the trees behind the farmhouse.

"Come on," she urged Perrin, who was sagging against her. "Let's go."

She didn't get more than ten steps before Murdina appeared in front of her. She held her sister against her and balled up a fist, her arm trembling with the effort. When had she become so weak? She'd always been the strong one. She had to stop giving into this crap and stand up for herself and Perrin.

"You're not taking her," she told the druidess.

"Neither shall you." Murdina's eyes opened wide, and shimmered with a strange light.

Rowan couldn't move, couldn't think, and

then she felt Perrin try to grab her. The light from the druidess's eyes filled her head, reaching down into her chest and seizing her heart in a glittering grip.

The ground rushed up at her face, and everything went black.

Chapter Twenty-Four

❦

ALTHEA KNEW SHE was dying. That wasn't her problem. She couldn't see properly out of her eyes anymore, and she couldn't blink, which she had never fully appreciated until she'd lost the ability to do so. Someone had helped her with the ice spears. One of the other women, she was sure of it. She just would have liked to know who before she died.

Maybe Emeline. She deserves an awesome power like that.

She watched Rowan try to get her sister away, only to be dropped by Murdina. Dha finally pulled the spear out of his head and tried to use it on Rowan, but the druidess stopped him. She murmured something to him, and he grabbed the sisters and stalked out of sight.

No blood on the spear, Althea noticed. The *famhair* didn't bleed, but from Dha's reaction to the spear in the eye, they felt pain. She wished she understood what that meant. She wished her eyes were clear, so she could see Brennus one last time when he came for her.

He would come too. She never doubted it for a moment.

I never got to tell you that I love you. I wish I'd done that.

Little black flecks fell in front of her frozen face, and then the tree trunk behind her began to shake. She wondered if it would fall over and crush her under it. That would be a faster death than this. Her heart thudded sluggishly in her chest as she saw a leaf growing beside her face. It came with a new greenish-brown branch, which curled around her neck. She was pretty sure that her legs had frozen solid, but she could hear something going on down there too. More branches appeared around her, and roots spread out on the ground beneath her.

I hope they bury me here, under this miracle of a tree.

Althea smiled inside as she watched the roots creep out in all directions. She put together a wild theory. Somehow the dead oak had started growing new limbs, which were covering her like a cocoon of thatching, and was sinking new roots into the ground. She might have been afraid—roots hadn't been her friends the last time she'd been here—but she had the strangest sense that she was being hugged, not attacked. As if the tree wanted to protect her.

You're a little too late for that.

Her body thawed a little under the cover of the armor of wooden branches, but she still couldn't feel anything. Her nerves had turned into ice, it seemed. She'd really done a number on herself by pouring her power out into the air like that.

It was really cool, though.

Giants came rushing out of the woods, their bodies impaled by the ice spears. They seemed to be in a big hurry. They grabbed Murdina and carried her off. Rowan and Perrin too.

Emeline stumbled toward her, and reached for the branches that were now sprouting thousands of new leaves. "Thank you, Althea. Thank you for trying. I'll never forget you."

She wouldn't either, Althea thought, and felt her lips crack as she managed a final smile. *Be good to yourself, Emeline—and stop dieting. You're beautiful the way you are.*

The nurse made it another couple of yards before one of the *famhairean* grabbed her and carried her off.

Althea heard the battle-cry of the Skar-aven, and looked toward the sound. Brennus would be at the very front of the riders, leading the charge. This was why she had hung on as long as she had. His face was the last one she wanted to see.

"Not mine?"

Althea looked into her Uncle Gene's eyes, the mirrors of her own, and felt her heart miss a beat. He was standing right in front of her, his Stetson pushed back on his head, his scuffed boots and faded jeans and plaid shirt exactly as she remembered. Only he hadn't been like that the last time she'd seen him, hooked up to machines in a hospital bed, his body being eaten alive by a bacterial infection with no cure. He'd gotten it when he'd cut his hand repairing some wire fencing. Necrotizing fasciitis had taken only four days to kill him.

"Now don't be like that, honey," he drawled. "It was my time to go. I had a good run. Had you to be my little girl. I should have managed a wife in there, but I never was a ladies' man." He reached out and rubbed his thumb over the tears frozen to her eyelashes. "That made you the love of my life, I reckon."

I've missed you so much, Uncle.

"You didn't give up, though, and that made me so proud. I've been watching over you, Althea Rose. You saved so many lives while you were here. Babies, and old folks, mothers and fathers, and more to come when they use your research. You were right about those ferns, honey. They're even going to squash that bug that did me in." His lean face grew serious. "You got a lot more to do."

But I'm dying.

"That's true enough," he said, nodding. "We all have to die. But our kind come back, Althea. We always come back." He checked the big chunky watch on his wrist. "It's my time now. I love you, honey."

Althea watched him fade away, just as her heartbeat was doing now. She heard the thunderous beat of horse's hooves, and saw through the leaves covering her face the first of the Skaraven burst out of the forest, driving dozens of giants back in a furious wave.

Brennus rode with his sword slicing through the air, through the *famhairean* falling away from him, their limbs severed. As dozens more rushed at him from the woods he wheeled about and roared, *"Fire."*

A hail of flaming arrows flew from the trees, striking the giants and setting them alight. They clawed away the shafts but the burning points melted into them, and fire blazoned out of the wounds. One by one the *famhairean* began to fall to their knees as their bodies went up in flames.

Hendry appeared on the other side of the encampment, and shouted at the few giants who hadn't been struck. "They use Pritani fire. We cannae fight them here. Leave with me, now."

The giants who could move fled from the

Skaraven, who still fought against those who burned with their unquenchable fire. From the charred remains that toppled, Althea saw the light of the giants' souls drift up, dragging something along with them.

The chieftain fought his way to the oak tree, but two giants nearly consumed by flame tried to drag him from his horse. His sword flashed as he cut them down, and then he leapt from his saddle to land in front of her.

"*Althea.*"

Now she could go. *I love you, I love you.* "I love you."

Her eyelids came down at last, and closed before the final beat of her heart.

Chapter Twenty-Five

A T TWILIGHT BRENNUS carried Althea's body up from the river and into Dun Mor. Behind him the clan herded their mounts and his to the stables Taran had rebuilt, where the Horse Master would see to watering and feeding them. He heard Cadeyrn issuing orders to the men to stand sentry and begin patrols. As tired and battered as they were, the clan made not a single complaint.

Inside the keepe Ruadri fetched a soft blanket and spread it over the table in his chamber, where Brennus stopped and looked down at his love's pale face. The frost and ice on her skin and eyes had melted away in the river, but her body remained stiff and unyielding.

Brennus looked blankly at the shaman. "I left her gown at McAra's."

"Taran went to fetch it after...after the battle, and gave it to me." Ruadri brought the emerald gown to the table. "Cadeyrn reports that the *famhairean* fled through a grove." When Brennus didn't reply, the shaman looked upon Althea for a long moment. "I'll leave you with her, and see to the burial."

Brennus nodded absently, and began unfastening her jacket.

Removing what she had brought with her from her time gave Brennus some comfort. She would go to her grave dressed as his lady wife. She became that the moment he tied his ring around her lovely neck. He would leave it with her, bury it with her, so that she remained his wife forever. Then he would have to find some reason to go on living.

There were many reasons, surely, but he could not recall one.

"I suspected they would see us coming for them," he told her as he eased the gown over her fiery hair. "'Twas why I had the men tip their arrows with Pritani fire. To burn them out of their bodies, and drive them into the trees. They cannot move in new forms until they are carved." He tugged the gown into place, and eased her over onto her side so he could tie the back laces. "'Twas meant to give us time to get you and the others out to the lochan."

Once he had dressed her, he found a comb and tended to her hair. He could do nothing about the bruise on her face, or the blackening of her ears and fingers, but they mattered not. When he looked at her he saw only her beauty.

"We've no more time, my lady," he said hoarsely. "I must part from you this day, and I cannae think of how I might." His voice dropped low. "How may I carry you to your rest, when you go without me? You vowed you would stay, but no' like this. How can you be gone from me?" He drew her up into his arms, and held her against him. "How could you die with words of love on your lips and no' hear mine?" He whispered into her hair.

"'Tis no' what I wanted. I had so much to tell you." His voice began to fail him. "So much."

Brennus held her like that for a long while. Too long, but his men left him alone to be with her. When he finally carried her out he saw they had fashioned a burial platform for her. Flowers covered every inch of it, and his men stood waiting on either side, ready to help carry her.

"She's mine," he told them, and put her atop the flowers. He lifted the platform from its middle, and the men moved aside, following him out of the keepe and into the night.

His sentries stood to light the path with their torches, and he followed the flames to a sheltered place where the clan had gathered. Cadeyrn stood in the deep grave, and cursed under his breath with the last shovelfuls he tossed from it. Kanyth helped him out, and the War Master looked at Brennus and Althea with a rage so wretched it nearly matched his own.

He felt his arms tremble.

"Help me with her," he asked his second.

Cadeyrn took the end of the platform with

shaking hands. Then dozens of others joined his, and the clan took her from him. They brought the platform over to the edge of the grave, and flowers tumbled down into the hollowed earth.

"Wait," Brennus said in a tight throat. He moved closer, and bent down to touch his quivering lips to hers. "I love you, my lady."

A flicker of dark light passed over his face, and as he drew back he saw that the clan ring she wore glowed blue. He scowled at it. Surely it had caught the moonlight, yet in all the years he'd worn it he'd never seen the like. But the more he stared at it, the brighter it glowed. He reached for it.

"What manner of–"

A tremendous blast shattered the night and threw him back. He landed atop Cadeyrn, and scrambled up to see every other Skaraven knocked off their feet, dozens of feet from the grave. As he helped his second to stand, he looked past him—at what could not be.

He ran.

Althea sat up as Brennus reached her, and linked her hands around his neck. Once he snatched her off the platform and into his arms, she touched her lips to his, murmuring his name as part of the kiss. He jerked back to look all over her. The bruise on her face, the black ice burns, all had vanished. Her hair glowed like burning copper and hung down to her waist, and in the moonlight her skin glowed as if polished with pearls.

"My lady," he murmured, when he could find his voice. He held her tightly, and covered the top of her head with kisses.

Cadeyrn shuffled over to them, staring without blinking, and then abruptly crumpled to the ground.

"Ruadri," Brennus called out. "We need a shaman over here."

The big man staggered to the War Master first. "He but fainted." He took slower steps to approach Althea, and held up his hand between them as the ink on his forearms glowed a pale blue. "You arenae dead, my lady."

"I'm not," she agreed but blinked at him. "Why?"

He swallowed. "I feel what you are, but I

cannae fathom it. 'Tis no' possible without a druid spell of great power."

Brennus reached out and grabbed the shaman's arm. "Never tell me she's awakened to immortality." When Ruadri nodded slowly he released him and looked at his love. "You did this."

"Maybe. I do have druid blood." She showed him his clan ring. "And this."

"We carved our clan rings from sacred oak, to protect us," the shaman said. "Bren, we were wearing the rings when we were awakened. They still contain the magic of the spell. Giving yours to your lady did the same for her."

The Skaraven began looking at each other with broad smiles.

"We didn't get the others back, did we?" Althea asked Brennus, and sighed when he shook his head. "We can't give up on them."

"We willnae, my lady." He pressed her slim hand over his heart. "We shall find them again, and rescue the ladies, and defeat the *famhairean*. I swear it."

"Then I think I can marry you," Althea said, and smiled at their clan. "It's time things changed for the Skaraven. I'm going to be part of that now. That means this clan is no longer male-only." She touched the ring again as she looked up at Brennus. "You don't mind, do you Chieftain?"

She laughed as he scooped her up in his arms and carried her back toward their home.

Chapter Twenty-Six

I N A SMALL room above a noisy village tavern, Oriana Embry sat and watched the images moving across the rough surface of Bhaltair Flen's bespelled crystal. The Skaraven Chieftain carried his laughing lady from an empty grave into a maze of ancient tors, followed by the rest of the clan.

"It doesnae show how we may find our way to Dun Mor, Master," she observed. "'Twould be better to ken where 'tis, so that in need we may call on the Skaraven directly."

"My dear one, the clan despises intruders almost as much as druid kind," Bhaltair said drily. "I wouldnae stray near the place even if it meant disincarnating."

Once the vision faded she rested her chin

on her hand. "But do you no' think it curious, Master, that a mere ring awakened the chieftain's lady love? 'Tis no' how our magic works."

"'Tis no longer our magic." The old druid picked up the crystal and carefully wrapped it in a protective linen. "The Skaraven possess their own power, through their battle spirits, unlike any of our talents. Now they live as immortals, and the lady came from druid kind."

Oriana got up to fetch him more evening brew. "'Tis no' so very bad. The Skaraven fought bravely against the *famhairean*. They'll keep searching for them until they're found and defeated. They vow to save the druidesses from the future."

"'Tis the stuff of conclavist nightmares." He rubbed a gnarled hand over his face. "You mustnae show such interest in their private matters. 'Tis unseemly. We're to have more dealings with the clan, and we must strive to be civil—and cautious."

"I shall in all things, Master." She offered a tentative smile. "I do hope you shall become their ally, like the McAra."

"If the Skaraven ever learn that we betrayed their plans to Hendry Greum," Bhaltair warned, "they shall gut us both and roast us on their spits." He winced. "'Tis to say, they shall never forgive us."

Her master had known that the message he'd left in his cottage would enrage the other druid. She and Bhaltair had rehearsed precisely what they would say in the presence of the flour.

Oriana braced her hands against the table, and heard Master Flen scrape back his chair as her eyes went white. Her grandfather's voice came from her lips, as clearly as if he were in the room. "Betrayal is something the Skaraven understand only too well, old friend."

Sneak Peek

Cadeyrn (Immortal Highlander, Clan Skaraven
Book 2)

Excerpt

CHAPTER ONE

Wedged in a corner beside a wooden bin, Lily
Stover listened to the winter wind wailing
outside the granary. Silly as it seemed, she
wished she knew what time and day it was.
Her watch had been smashed during her last
beating, and calendars probably hadn't yet
been invented in fourteenth-century Scotland.
At least the bitterly cold gusts couldn't get at

her in her new medieval prison. The storage building's thick stone walls had no windows, and something heavy barred the only door from the outside. For that she should be grateful, as she had only the damp, dirty clothes on her back and her sodding safety shoes, which had started to come apart at the seams.

As long as her mind didn't do the same she'd be aces.

Staying alive didn't make her heart glow with gratitude. These last weeks she'd been subjected to malicious beatings, beastly conditions, and constant starvation. Her entire body felt like one great minging bruise. Working double shifts as a sous-chef in the Atlantia Princess's busy, cramped galley had never left her feeling this filthy or knackered. If by some staggering stroke of luck she ever made it back to the twenty-first century, she was never again stepping one foot off that bloody cruise ship.

"Can we eat this, Lily?"

She looked up at Emeline, the black-haired Scottish nurse who had been taken with her and the two Thomas sisters. Throughout their ordeal she'd looked after everyone without complaint, even ignoring her own wrenched shoulder and badly-bruised jaw to tend to their injuries.

Since they had no food, her question perplexed Lily. "What are you on about?" The hoarse sound of her own voice made her stomach surge, and she tried again. "Sorry. You've found food?"

"Maybe." Emeline raised the lid of the wooden bin and scooped out a handful of grain to show her. "I think it's wheat, but I'm not sure." She glanced over her shoulder at the sisters before she murmured, "Perrin hasn't eaten for days."

Perrin Thomas, the older of the sisters, sat on the floor staring at nothing. A professional dancer, she'd been slender from the start. She'd lost at least a stone since they'd arrived, whittling her delicate features and long limbs to a skeletal gauntness.

"She'll do better." Lily had talked to her last night about that and several other things, and the dancer had promised to try to eat enough to keep up her strength. "Let's have a look at the grain."

Lily inspected the kernels, which had been winnowed to remove the indigestible hull. She sifted her fingers through it to look for rot or mold, and then popped a grain in her mouth to chew it. The nutty flavor confirmed what it was. "It's barley, but it looks all right." She squinted at the nurse's swollen jaw. "Soaking it for an hour will make it softer."

Emeline gave her a lopsided smile. "No water yet."

No water. No food. No blankets or medicines or bandages or help. The nurse always tagged her inventories of their deprivations with that optimistic word— *yet*—but she knew as well as Lily what they couldn't depend on: hope.

A pair of golden ducat eyes, burning like cognac flambé, glared at her from her memory. They belonged to the nameless Scottish warrior who had tried to rescue her at the mountain sheep farm. When Lily had been snatched out of his reach and carried off, he'd let out a roar of fury that still echoed in her head. He'd kept riding after her, up to the moment when the mad druids had forced them into the portal and brought them here.

He hadn't given up on her, and neither would she—not yet.

"Pound it with a stone first, to break up the kernels into smaller bits. Should be easier to swallow." When Emeline nodded and went back to the sisters, Lily dumped the grain in the bin, and leaned her head back and closed her eyes.

She knew she should try and eat, but reliving those precious few seconds she'd seen the man with the strange, glowing tattoo on his arm gave her the only comfort she'd known since being snatched from the outdoor market.

Unfortunately, other, uglier memories decided to come first.

The day before she'd been taken, Lily had received a vile letter from her father's solicitor, sternly informing her that she'd been disinherited. Gourmet restaurateur and food magazine publisher Edgar Stover had reluctantly revealed that she, Lily Elizabeth Stover, wasn't his biological child. Of course, as a bastard she had no claims to financial provision under Britain's Inheritance Act of 1975. She was, unequivocally, cut off without a pound from the wealthiest epicure in the UK.

Through the rest of her shift Lily had smiled. When one of the pastry chefs had asked her what was so amusing, she'd laughed and said, "I'm penniless."

To celebrate after work, she'd taken a demi of champagne back to her cabin to drink. Then she'd been sick, but even chundering half the night had felt glorious. At last she'd been freed. Edgar would never have her dragged back to London now. The drinking binge and her almost-delirious happiness had made her reckless. The next morning she'd asked for shore leave for the first time in six months. The head chef had agreed, with the condition that she buy some local produce for him. She'd practically skipped down the gangway to the dock at Invergordon.

Lily opened her eyes, but she couldn't stop seeing the rest. Renting a scooter and riding out into the country had been such fun. She'd stopped at a small farmers' market where she'd found the sweetest gooseberries she'd ever sampled. Then the earth had exploded around her, and a huge thing shaped like a cracked-faced plastic rugby player had grabbed her by the neck.

Her trembling hand went right to her throat, and she swallowed a mouthful of bile. Those unspeakable moments should have been blurry, but instead they'd been etched on her brain. The thing had dragged her like a carcass toward the hole in the ground. The sickening crack of bones. The silent screaming inside her head when she'd realized what he had done to her. How with one blow the thing had bashed in the head of an old farmer who had tried to save her. Then being pulled underground, and through the ground, only to be hurled into another pit filled with thrashing branches. When she'd finally landed in the fourteenth century, somehow she'd staggered to her feet to run. The thing had caught her again, and tried to strangle her before another one pushed it away.

You cannae kill this one. The Wood Dream need all five.

The scraping, groaning sound outside the granary brought Lily to her feet. Emeline quickly hauled Perrin away from the door, while the dancer's younger sister, Rowan came to stand in front of it. The slushy ground outside slopped as footsteps approached, and then a thin, middle-aged man with silver-streaked dark hair and viper-green eyes stepped inside.

"Good morning, sisters." Hendry Greum tucked his hands behind his back, making his voluminous robe sway as he surveyed them all. "I trust you slept well?"

"With no blankets, food, or water?" Rowan snarled back at him. "How do you think?"

Emeline came to stand beside the carpenter, and touched her shoulder before she said to Hendry, "We're injured and exhausted, but with some proper food and rest we'll recover. If you continue the kind of abuse we suffered at the forest farm, I doubt any of us will survive the week."

The druid nodded. "Until last night I wasnae aware of how badly your conditions became. You shall be given the provisions and care you require, but first I'll need something in return."

Rowan tensed and leaned forward. "We don't have—"

"Quiet," Emeline snapped, silencing the carpenter as she pulled her back. Calmly, she turned to Hendry. "What do you want?"

"One of you has a new talent." He scanned their faces like a hungry fox inside a full coop. "A talent used to help Althea Jarden during the Skaraven attack. That caused injury to many of our *caraidean*, and that I willnae have. Tell me who has the mind-move gift, and the three who didnae help our enemy shall be well-treated and kept safe."

Rowan made a rude sound. "Like we're going to fall for that. The minute you leave the beatings and starvation will start all over again."

"I've no plans to leave," the druid told her. "But should I need to, I'll leave Ochd with orders to stand guard over you."

Perrin rose to her feet and walked up to Hendry. "So all we have to do is give you the collaborator, and the rest of us get to live? We'll really be safe?"

"You have my word on it," the druid said.

The dancer backed away from him, and then turned around to point at Lily. "It was her. She's the one who can move things with her mind."

• • • • •

Buy *Caderyn (Immortal Highlander, Clan Skaraven Book 2)* Now

DO ME A FAVOR?

You can make a big difference.

Reviews are the most powerful tools I have when it comes to getting attention for my books. Much as I'd like it, I don't have the financial muscle of a New York publisher. I can't take out full page ads in the newspaper— not yet, anyway.

But I do have something much more powerful. It's something that those publishers would kill for: **a committed and loyal group of readers.**

Honest reviews of my books help bring them to the attention of other readers. If you've enjoyed this book I would so appreciate it if you could spend a few minutes leaving a review—any length you like.

Thank you so much!

MORE BOOKS BY HH

For a complete, up-to-date book list, visit
HazelHunter.com/books.

Get notifications of new releases and special
promotions by joining my newsletter!

Glossary

Here are some brief definitions to help you navigate the medieval world of the Immortal Highlanders.

acolyte - novice druid in training
Am Monadh Ruadh - the original Scots Gaelic name for the Cairngorm mountains, which translates to English as "the red hills"
aye - yes
bairn - child
bastart - bastard
baws - balls, testicles
Beinn Nibheis – old Scots Gaelic for Ben Nevis, the highest mountain in Scotland
blaeberry - European fruit that resembles the American blueberry

blethering - chatting

bleezin' -drunk

blind - cover device

blood kin - genetic relatives

boon - gift or favor

Bràithrean an fhithich - Brethren of the raven

brieve - a writ

brilliant - British slang for excellent or marvelous

buckler - shield

bugger - British slang for a contemptible person

cac - Scots gaelic for "shit"

Caledonia - ancient Scotland

cannae - can't

caraidean - Scots Gaelic for "friends"

Chieftain - the head of a specific Pritani tribe

clout - strike

comely - attractive

conclave - druid ruling body

conclavist - member of the druid ruling body

couldnae - couldn't

cow - derogatory term for woman

croft - small rented farm

cudgel - wooden club

daft - crazy

dinnae - don't

disincarnate - commit suicide

doesnae - doesn't

dru-wid - Proto Celtic word; an early form of "druid"

eagalsloc - synonym for "oubliette"; coined from Scots Gaelic for "fear" and "pit"; an inescapable hole or cell where prisoners are left to die

ell - ancient unit of length measurement, equal to approximately 18 inches

fack - fuck

facking - fucking

famhair - Scots Gaelic for giant (plural, famhairean)

fathom - understand

feart - Scottish or Irish for afraid

firesteel - a piece of metal used with flint to create sparks for fire-making

Francia - France

Francian - French

Gaul - ancient region that included France, Belgium, southern Netherlands, southwestern Germany, and northern Italy

Germania - Germany

goosed - Scottish slang for "smashed"

greyling - species of freshwater fish in the salmon family

hasnae - hasn't

Hispania - Roman name for the Iberian peninsula (modern day Portugal and Spain)

incarnation - one of the many lifetimes of a druid

isnae - isn't

keeker - black eye

ken - know

lad - boy

laird - lord

larder - pantry

lass - girl

league - distance measure of approximately three miles

leannan - Scots Gaelic for "beloved"

lochan - a small lake

magic folk - druids

mayhap - maybe

mustnae - must not

naught - nothing

no' - not

NOSAS - North of Scotland Archaeology Society

oubliette - a dungeon with an opening only at
the top

ovate - Celtic priest or natural philosopher

Pritani - Britons (one of the people of
southern Britain before or during Roman
times)

quim - woman's genitals

quisling - a traitor who collaborates with
the enemy

reeks like an alky's carpet - very smelly

ruddy - a British intensifier and euphemism
for bloody

shouldnae - shouldn't

skelp - strike, slap, or smack

slee - sly, cunning

solar - rooms in a medieval castle that served
as the family's private living and sleeping
quarters

spew - vomit

staunch weed - yarrow

Tha mi a 'gealltainn - Scots Gaelic for "I
promise"

'tis - it is

'tisnt - it isn't

tor - large, freestanding rock outcrop

tree-knower - the Skaraven nickname for the druids of their time

trencher - wooden platter for food

trews - trousers

'twas - it was

'twere - it was

'twill - it will

'twould - it would

uisge beatha - old Scots Gaelic for "whiskey"

undercroft - a room in a lower level of a castle used for storage

vole - small rodent related to the mouse

wasnae - wasn't

watchlight - a term for a grease-soaked rush stalk, used as a candle in medieval times

wee - small

wench - girl or young woman

willnae - will not

wouldnae - would not

Pronunciation Guide

A selection of the more challenging words in the Immortal Highlander, Clan Skaraven series.

Ailpin - ALE-pin
Althea Jarden - al-THEE-ah JAR-den
Am Monadh Ruadh - im monih ROOig
Aon - OOH-wen
Beinn Nibheis - ben NIH-vis
Bhaltair Flen - BAHL-ter Flen
Black Cuillin - COO-lin
Bràithrean an fhithich - BRAH-ren ahn
EE-och
Brennus Skaraven - BREN-ess skah-RAY-ven
Bridei - BREE-dye

cac - kak

Cailean Lusk - KAH-len Luhsk

Caderyn - KAY-den

caraidean - KAH-rah-deen

Coig - COH-egg

Dha - GAH

eagalsloc - EHK-al-slakh

Emeline McAra - EM-mah-leen mac-CAR-ah

famhair - FAV-ihr

Ferath - FAIR-ahth

Galan - gal-AHN

Gwyn Embry - gah-WIN AHM-bree

Hendry Greum - HEN-dree GREE-um

Kanyth - CAN-ith

Kelturan - KEL-tran

Lily Stover - LILL-ee STOW-ver

lochan - LOHK-an

Maddock McAra - MAH-duck mac-CAR-ah

Manath - MAN-ahth

Murdina Stroud - mer-DEE-nah STROWD

Ochd - OHK

Oriana Embry - or-ree-ANN-ah AHM-bree

Perrin Thomas - PEAR-in TOM-us

Rowan Thomas - ROW-en TOM-us

Ruadri - roo-ah-DREE

Taran - ter-RAN

Tha mi a 'gealltainn - HA mee a GYALL-ting

Tri - TREE

uisge beatha - OOSH-ka bah

Dedication

For Mr. H.

Copyright

Made in the USA
Columbia, SC
30 May 2018